"You'll learn to be happy in your new home, but only when you shed those awful people, those malefactors from your soul," Warren assured, before exiting.

In all my life I'd never felt as defeated as I did in that moment. No plan. No means to an end. Nothing. This psychopath intended on keeping me here forever. Who knew what "precautions" he had in play to prevent anyone from leaving? Invisible electric fence? Armed whacko guards? Poison?

She Without Sin

by

JP Barry

The Fall of Winters Trilogy

She Without Sin

Cover Art by *Debbie Taylor*

The Wild Rose Press, Inc.
PO Box 708
Adams Basin, NY 14410-0708
Visit us at www.thewildrosepress.com

Publishing History
First Edition, 2024
Trade Paperback ISBN 978-1-5092-5144-5
Digital ISBN 978-1-5092-5145-2

The Fall of Winters Trilogy
Published in the United States of America
Previously Published 2020 MuseItUp Publishing

Dedication

For my husband & daughter - Everything is limitless, especially you.

Chapter 1

Nick

There's something to be said about the lifespan of a marriage. Of course, everything begins with this moronic, idyllic, blissful sentiment imbibed with foolish hope – something one wishes to bottle, uncorking at precisely the right moment when things go south, because they *always* do. However, that first Hollywood style "meet-cute" will cloud your brain with consuming lustful thoughts, obscuring your otherwise good judgement. Raging hormones will trick you into believing Cupid's arrow struck your heart. Stabbed it is more like it. From that day forward, you're screwed – royally. For a select few, the happily-ever-after nonsense we're conditioned to seek and foster actually occurs, but for most, it doesn't. *And*, I've got news for you – it never will.

So, there you sit, in a cold, dimly lit conference room of an overpriced legal group fighting over who gets what. Suddenly, a gaudy set of priceless dishes you inherited from a relative you couldn't stand when they were alive will cost you ten thousand dollars, forty phone calls, dozens of emails, and heartburn that radiates from your kneecaps, because for some reason you both have to have it to spite the other. Each of you is painfully aware the crap will end up in a box at a local thrift shop or tossed to the curb on trash day, but anger is a funny emotion causing even the most level-headed to lose the plot. I, myself, used to be a calm minded man – that was until I met my soon-to-be ex-wife.

"My client demands the main family house. We will not bend, nor break, on this mutual asset. Mr. Winters is more than welcome to sole ownership of their vacation home in Cape Cod. Both properties have been assessed at roughly the same value. It's more-or-less an even exchange. We attest the give-and-take to be fair," Charles Downey informed. The beanpole with impeccable posture irritated the hell out of me. Whenever he'd open his mouth to speak, that whiney voice incited a rage so dark and deep I couldn't see clearly. Aside from costing a fortune a second for his services, the fact he was on Jillian's side made him the enemy – a force I'd need to beat into oblivion.

"First, it's *Doctor* Winters, not *Mr.* Winters. I believe I earned that title, *and* the respect which goes along with it. Second, I paid for that house, Jill. When we got it, you were doing the farm report at three in the morning for that nobody-ever-watches station," I shot back, not waiting for my lawyer to speak up. Had fury not been fueling my thoughts, the words might've been less heated. Most times I could've cared less if someone referred to me as Mr. Winters instead of Doctor Winters. The validation to feel intellectually superior to those around me wasn't required. I knew who and what I was, and was acutely aware of the hard work it took to get there. Others didn't have to recognize it for a sense of internal justness. Despite what Jillian thought, my ego wasn't the size of Texas, but rather constantly in check. Hers, well you'd need three universes to fully cage the damn thing. However, at this point, I was simply being an asshole for the hell of it.

Truth is, way back when Jillian and I began, she held reputable employment at a small, local network. Jillian was paying her dues, as so many of us have. I'd encouraged her to not see the stepping stone as a crap job, but to own it, being the best beat reporter the station ever had, which she did.

"The *farm report*, huh." Jillian smirked, leaning across the table. "Listen to me, you pompous, arrogant jackass. You bought nothing, *Doctor* Winters. Your parents purchased that home as a wedding present – a present *you* didn't want, so *you* put the property in *my* name, therefore it's *mine*. Not *yours*. *And*, let's not forget who makes more money now. It belongs to me. Do you understand the words coming out of my mouth, or should I break it down into smaller, more manageable sentences?"

"Oh? You want to play *that* game. Awesome. Here we go. Who carried you all those years when you were making less than a teenager working at a fast-food restaurant? Me. That's who. Who stimulated you to keep going when you wanted to quit? That's right. Me, again. But, my favorite bit of information – who introduced you to Liam? One more time for the hearing impaired – me. If it wasn't for *me* and *my* family name, you'd still be nobody. If I want the damn house, I will take it regardless of what you want or think. Do *you* understand, or should *I* simplify it for *you*?" In all my years walking this Earth I'd never seen red, unless Jillian was close by. That woman could scare the crap out of the Devil himself. She'd pick at weaknesses, poking and prodding until whomever the target was exploded. Maybe that was her endgame – who knew. Perhaps it's a power trip of sorts. The woman was tremendously skilled at it. She could teach a masters level class on it. The sad part of the entire situation? Jillian had been the farthest thing from a bitch years ago. The change had been slight with each passing day. I didn't realize until the end.

Standing abruptly, I crashed my chair against the hardwood floor. My fists balled tightly to the point my knuckles turned white as my chest heaved with ire.

Challenge me. Challenge me, Jill, and I swear I'll tear you apart. I dare you. Come on, wifey.

Part of me wanted this fight – a battle to the death, but another part, no matter how awful Jillian had grown, still recalled with precise clarity the beautiful, wide-eyed, innocent girl she once was. We met at Princeton, literally running into each other outside the Firestone Library. She was headed out. I was going in. Hurriedly, she collected her fallen books, mumbled a few inaudible utterances, and rushed off, not paying any mind to the situation at hand. I, however, was blown away by her ethereal looks. The weeks which proceeded were spent desperately searching for my mystery woman, but she'd vanished. Finally, one freezing cold winter evening in a bar off campus, I spotted her sitting with some people at a table a few yards away. A buddy of mine knew her from class. After much persuading, he agreed to introduce us.

Jillian Locke – journalism major. The combination of her long, bouncy, curled, shiny auburn hair, sapphire eyes, toned body, sun kissed smooth skin, and subtle expressions grabbed me by the balls, not letting up until she became mine. Despite her divine physical appearance, Jillian was brilliant. She was able to speak on any topic for hours. She was well-read and traveled, cultured, but above all kind, warm, and loving, emotions I wasn't familiar with coming from the over-privileged political Winters Family.

Ah, yes, the Winters Clan. Politicians since the dawn of time. Well, all except me – the proverbial black sheep. I went into psychology, which damn near almost killed dear 'ole Mom and Dad – Mister Speaker of the House, Tag Winters, and his dutiful wife, Miranda, a retired superintendent of schools who hadn't seen the inside of a classroom in well over forty years. My grandfather, former Vice President Beau Winters, was probably the most liked politician of all time. Beau boldly crossed party lines showing the country what true bipartisanship meant – extending a hand across the aisle for the greater good of his country. He stood by what was fair, not by what his party wanted. My grandfather not only listened to his constituents, he heard them, often being the voice of reason during turbulent times. The country loved and adored the way he spoke, and how he took immediate action. Unfortunately, his run for President was cut short after he suffered a massive heart attack. Putting family and health first, he stepped back, working behind the scenes by helping my siblings and cousins break into the political rat race. When I told him I wanted to become a psychologist, he and my grandmother were the only two who supported the career choice.

"You're doing the right thing, Nicky. Follow your heart. You'll be far happier. Politics isn't the type of life I want for you. Go help people. Heal and unite them in ways I never could. I'm proud of you, my boy," Grandfather whispered in my ear as I left to return to school after sophomore Spring Break.

To date, my older sister, Savannah, is a distinguished Congresswoman from Connecticut. My other older sister, Morgan, is a Senator from Connecticut. And, my older brother, Jackson, also a Senator, but from Maryland, is currently attempting to run for President. The baby of the group, me, Nicholas Winters, wanted nothing to do with any of it. Still don't. Politicians were all liars, thieves, and shady scam artists. They made empty promises to the public feeling no remorse when they didn't deliver on the goods. That's not who I am. Frankly, it's never been, nor ever will be, no matter how angry I might become. My mother and father may be icebox parents, but freezing people out is a great way to show the world you're nothing but a giant jerk.

I stumbled across psychology after having been exposed to it myself for many years as an adolescent. A short temper was always my problem, often earning me a trip to the Head Master's office. My parents, tired of having to run to the school to clean up my mess, embarrassed I was tainting the good Winters name, slammed my ass in therapy, pressuring the psychologist to "*fix me*" as fast as humanly possible. Armed with firsthand knowledge of the positive benefits of counseling, I knew I'd found where I belonged. Today, I was a wildly popular, number one bestselling self-help author, and host the most listened to podcast in the country. I hadn't seen patients in years and missed it tremendously, but with a larger platform I'd been afforded the ability to aid more people on a broader scale.

"I wonder how your fans would feel about you

threatening your wife," Jillian replied calmly, leaning back in her chair, and crossing arms and legs. You didn't need to have a degree in reading body language to realize the movement clearly showed self-protection against me.

"If they knew the real you, they'd understand," I clapped back.

"Pot or kettle, Nick? Let's not travel down the road of what's fact and what's fiction."

"Why do you want the house so bad? You can afford to buy yourself a new one."

"So can you." Her face knotted with wrath.

"Your acute case of resting bitch face doesn't scare me, Jill. I'm immune," I said, in response to the harsh expression.

"It should," she warned.

"Mr. Downey, would your client be willing to sell the property?" my attorney, Matthew Miller, asked with a great, long sigh. His chubby fingertips tapped the white marble tabletop while he shifted impatiently in his seat. I had no idea why this man appeared rushed, caring about how much time we spent arguing when he was paid by the hour, and handsomely, might I add.

Downey leaned closer to Jillian feverishly whispering in her ear. "No," he replied, returning to his natural seated position.

"God damn it!" I shouted out of frustration. "It's like you get off on being difficult. You've been like this our entire marriage. Enough already. We're shelling out hundreds of thousands of dollars to lawyers for what? A frigging house neither of us like or truly want? For Christ's sake, winning isn't everything. Fine. Take the frigging house. It's yours. Everything I own is yours. Happy now?" My hands aggressively ran through my hair. If I could've yanked it out, I would've. She'd pushed me to my absolute limit.

"Do you see what I've had to deal with?" Jillian said to both attorneys, throwing her arms in the air.

"What *you've* had to deal with? Surely you can't be serious. What about what *I've* had to endure? What about all of the affairs? Didn't think I knew about your side pieces? I've seen the countless trash rag stories and have witnessed the station's pathetic attempts at covering the disgusting acts up. Don't make me laugh. You're a disgrace and embarrassment."

Ha! Put that in your pipe and smoke it, Jill.

An "if looks could kill" mien drew across Jillian's face as she glared at me. Our eyes locked in hatred. For a moment, those two bold sapphires captivated me. This primal caveman beast from within me craved taking hold of her slender waist, shoving all of the papers and folders on the table aside, slamming her ass down on it, and doing her like she'd never been done before.

"This meeting is over," Jillian said. A lone tear rolled down her cheek, leaving a trail of smudged rose blush behind. Her head turned away quickly to hide the demonstrative surge.

"Jill, babe. Come on. Please, don't cry." I exhaled, walking to her. I'd pushed her too far and that wasn't okay.

"Like you really give a crap," she sniffed. Her insinuation hurt. Yeah, sure, I was pissed beyond measure, but I never meant to wound her to the point of breaking down. An instant sense of pain consumed my heart. The ego I thought to be in check wasn't in the least.

"Would it be possible to have a moment alone with my wife?" I asked the two lawyers.

After exchanging a glance, they nodded, exiting the space along with a stenographer and two legal secretaries. Once the door clicked shut, I reached for her arms, pulling her to her feet. Call it a moment of weakness or momentary insanity, but seeing her weep, something she rarely did, crushed my soul. I had to heal her, and make her feel whole again.

"I'm sorry. You're not a disgrace, nor an embarrassment. No matter how irritated I may be, it's never okay to speak to anyone the way I just did, especially when it's you."

"I can't do this right now, Nick." Raising her right hand to stop the conversation, she shook her head before turning away. This was a classic Jillian Winters defense mechanism. Whenever anything became too real, avoidance became her favorite go-to move.

"It doesn't have to be like this, Jill. We don't have to end our story here, but I can't do it alone," I reasoned. The fact she didn't storm out of the room ranting proved to be a strong, positive sign. With an abundance of caution, my fingers slowly slid up her shoulders. Gently turning her body, I applied soft pressure to her chin in order to gain face-to-face contact.

Jillian didn't resist the forced movement; however, my words were met with silence, but a warm silence. Not her typical subzero kind. The wheels inside of her head were turning. She hadn't fully completed the comprehension process, yet. It appeared the severity of our reality finally hit her. A floodgate of tears poured down her face, falling onto my forearms.

"We can start over, but drastic changes must be made. For starters, we should go to marriage counseling – work through our issues, because there's a lot of them.

Our communication sucks. It wasn't always like that, but in recent years we've given up on talking and connecting." Tenderly, my fingertips brushed moisture from her face. Her cheek turned into the touch.

"I own my mistakes, Nick. I admit to not always treating you well or with fairness and respect, *but* I wasn't the only one who stepped outside of our marriage. You started the cycle with *Kelly*. Focus has never been on you, always me and my screw-ups. I'm made out to be this awful, horrible creature, while you're off in left field, out of the direct line of fire, playing the role of the battered husband. We both know that's not the entire truth, yet my character is the only one getting publicly slammed. I've had to work my ass off to get to where I am, and yes, I had to piss a lot of people off to get here, but I don't regret being forceful," she whispered.

The sound of my former lover's name caused discomfort to shoot through my chest. Kelly was a mistake. An epic error of devastating proportion. Though the happening occurred over the span of a half a decade, she'd been it – the only other woman. When it ended, I swore I'd never do it again, and I haven't.

Kelly Greenly was my ex-personal assistant. She was a young, pretty, intelligent woman, but more importantly, she was available at a time when I needed that most. The moment Jillian's career took off, she threw herself into it giving one hundred ten percent of herself. I, too, proved guilty of the same, going full force with promoting my work, traveling ten out of the twelve-month calendar year. As a therapist I should've seen the signs – they were there, clear as day, but out of loneliness, the need to feel desired, attractive, powerful, and sheer horniness while on tour, I ended up sleeping with her. I hadn't been with another woman since marrying Jillian, so the different experience became an addiction – one I couldn't seem to kick no matter how hard I tried.

Long story short, Jillian decided to surprise me when I was in New Orleans. The front desk clerk recognized her and stupidly handed over my room key – no questions asked. Had Kelly and I not been in bed together, the unexpected visit would've been welcomed, but unfortunately, that's not how the situation turned out. The odd thing, the thing I should've dug deeper into, was the fact Jillian refused to acknowledge the occurrence. She left without uttering a single word, and when I finally spoke with her – several days later because I'm a jerk who's too scared to face the harsh reality of infidelity, she acted as if nothing happened; business as usual. Not wanting to address my fault, rock the preverbal boat, I played along, promptly breaking things off with Kelly, who wasn't thrilled over it. After a quick, late-night SOS call to my grandfather, he arranged for my dirty little secret to go away. Since that day, I haven't seen or heard from her.

My new assistant, Don, promptly began work the following week. However, not everything that came from my error in judgement turned out bad. Something valuable was realized from my imprudence. I recognized how much I truly loved Jillian and didn't want anyone else. When her affairs came to light, I showed no reaction, though a small piece of me died each time I read a rag magazine article about one. Addressing it would've been the pot calling the kettle black.

"You're right. I should've forced you to open a dialogue about it. I should've owned what I did. I can't imagine how you must've felt. Well, actually, I can. Probably the same way I did when I found out about your indiscretions, *but* we're not talking about that. We're discussing how *I* hurt *you*. I'm a therapist. You're my wife. I should've known better. I'm sorry, Jill. From the bottom of my soul, I'm sorry." I paused to make sure our eyes remained locked. "Please, believe me. If I could do it all over again, I swear I wouldn't have touched her. You're my everything, whereas I never gave a damn about her, and never will. I failed you, and in turn, out of hurt and anger, you struck back. I deserved that, but I'm willing to leave all this in the past if you're willing to as well. I love you, Jill. Tell me how I can prove that to you. Whatever it takes. Just think about this before we pull the trigger on terminating us."

"I don't see how that's possible, Nick," she said, still maintaining eye contact – a durable indication her heart and mind were searching for a solution to our current dilemma, but was struggling to do so.

"I do. We withdraw the petition for divorce and go back to square one – remembering why we fell in love in the first place. We do that by getting to know the other again. Perhaps we take a vacation, or simply go out on a few dates. Whatever you're comfortable with. We'll actively put our best foot forward and take time off from work. It won't be easy, but the station can survive without you, and the needy, emotionally wounded people of the world will be just fine in my absence for a little while. I'll find another shrink to cover the show and will place the second part of the book tour on pause. Our sleeping arrangement can stay the same – you in our room, me in the guest room, but instead of passing the other in the hallway without saying a word, we talk. We make a point of it to set time aside each day to open an active, calm dialogue. Many conversations will be rough and uncomfortable, others not so much, but if we want this, we'll get through the bumpy patch together, and be better for it. If in three months we can't seem to move on, we can re-file with the courts, and pick up where we left off. In the interim, we go slow and rebuild, together. Do you want this, Jill? Do you want us? Are you willing to fight for us?"

"A half hour ago you were ready to strangle me, Nick. Why the sudden change of heart?" Her head tilted to the right as her left eyebrow raised. She had suspicions I was up to something. Maybe I was, but that didn't mean I wasn't speaking the truth about wanting to give our marriage one more shot.

"If something still hurts, that means you still care. This is killing me. Seeing you cry – I just can't, Jill. Never could. You know this. Tell me you're not in any form of pain and I won't believe you. This isn't us. We're better than the way we've been acting to ourselves and each other."

"I hate what we've become." She sniffed, leaning into my chest, waiting to see if I'd embrace her or not.

Wrapping both of my arms around her waist, I held her tightly. "Me too, babe. Come on. Let's go home. Tomorrow is a new day. We've got a lot to sort out."

"Okay," she replied with a deep sigh, accepting my comfort.

Exhaling deeply, I wasn't sure if we'd be able to work things out, but I was sure the part of me that loved her still existed. Only time would tell if we were all in or not. That would have to be enough for now.

Chapter 2

Jillian

Tiny flecks of gold breached the plantation shutters inside of the master bedroom casting shadows on the ivory Egyptian cotton comforter. In last night's haste, I'd forgotten to completely shut them. Rolling onto my side, I saw Nick sleeping on his back. His one arm was positioned above his head; the top sheet draped carelessly over his waist exposing his chest and legs. In spite of our current shit storm, he was still the most brilliant, handsome, devastatingly attractive man I'd ever known. Perfectly cropped salt and pepper hair complimented his deep olive skin. Bright emerald eyes and a killer, megawatt smile added to his allure. Based off his thick biceps, tree trunk toned thighs, six-pack abs, and deep inguinal creases, one would never guess he was close to fifty years old. He'd always been a sharp, classy dresser, but now armed with a wallet full of his own money, his style was untouchable. His laugh – heart stopping.

Standing in the lawyer's office an entire host of sentiments crashed together in one loud mental explosion. The sharp one-hundred-eighty-degree turn taken within a matter of thirty minutes caused me emotional whiplash. I supposed, if I really thought about it for a hot second, deep down, buried beneath years of hurt, vindictiveness, and anger I didn't want this divorce. Neither did Nick. When he called for a truce, relief rose to the surface. The tough as nails exterior I'd always worn as impenetrable armor comfortably dropped. At the heart of the matter, I wasn't anything at all like the media portrayed me. However, with most celebrities two personas existed, always, side by side. On air, Jillian Winters was a bitch. Rough, hard, unrelenting, powerful, and unstoppable. Off air Jill was quiet, reserved, and most times scared of what might be. Years ago Nick often referred to me as his "shy fierceness." A total oxymoron, but rather fitting.

After apprehensively leaving the lawyer's office, we decided to have a quiet dinner back at our house. Nick ordered in from our favorite Italian restaurant – a place we hadn't gone to in forever. Between time restrictions, work commitments, and the overall breakdown of us, who had the will or want to share a meal? In fact, I couldn't remember when we last sat at the table and did anything together. As foreign as it felt, tonight we did. Honestly? Most of the conversations sucked. They were uncomfortable, but never-the-less, necessary. Over coffee I realized if we could get through the first of what would probably end up being many ugly discussions, we'd be okay. There'd been no yelling or screaming like in the past, only talking and active listening. Words were absorbed and processed, not ignored and unheard. Nick wasn't wrong about my affairs acting his punishment. A large part of me wanted to wound him the same way he'd destroyed me; make him experience the tearing ache inside of his heart. Truthfully, I had no emotions or feelings for any of the men I'd been with. They were warm revenge bodies in retaliation of *Kelly*, the office slut. The thought of her made my stomach clench in disgust. After each tryst with the flavor of the moment, I'd loathe myself over the act I committed. A tiny part of me would temporarily feel satisfied I'd struck Nick where it counted, but when the emotion left, I'd returned to a state of emptiness, revolted I'd sunk to such a new low. That behavior wasn't who I was, nor what I stood for, but the memory of him in bed with Kelly haunted me in ways I never knew existed.

After cleaning the kitchen, I set the timer on the coffeemaker for seven the following morning. Nick approached me from behind, firmly taking hold of my waist.

"You're so damn sexy," he murmured, pressing his hips into my behind. "This is against the rules, I'm aware, but I can't help myself, babe, mainly because I don't want to. If you're uncomfortable, I'll stop. Just say the word."

"Nick," I whispered breathy, caught somewhere between wanting to give in and being unsure if this was the best move. Five hours ago, we sat in an attorney's office ready to call it quits, but we agreed to give us time to work through things. However, that didn't mean jumping into bed together after months of separation and quarreling. Inhaling to regain my lost composure, his heady smell invaded my leveled good sense, clouding any and all better judgement.

"I'm sorry, Jill. You're not ready and that's more than okay. I understand. With time I hope we can find our way back to being intimate, not just sexually, but in other aspects too. Meanwhile, I'll patiently wait, because you're worth it and deserve better than me acting like a pig," he said, kissing my bare shoulder and taking a step away, providing me with ample personal space.

In a split-second, ill-informed decision, I pivoted, grabbed hold of his wrist, pulling him back, and crushing our lips together. The physical contact reminded how much I missed his touch. Like teenagers, we went at it all over the house, finally ending in our room. How the day could start at a divorce lawyer's office and end in bed with the man you wanted to murder less than a day ago blew my mind.

"Where are you, Jill?" Nick asked, quietly turning on his side. His thick fingers reached out and stroked my thigh.

"Right here," I replied.

"I'm aware." He chuckled. "What I meant was, what are you thinking about? Talk to me."

"Work," I lied, because I didn't feel like opening Pandora's Box so early in the morning without coffee.

"I see. Would you like to unpack that bag a bit more? Please, Jill. Let me in."

Propping himself up on his right arm, he made direct eye contact while raising one perfectly manicured brow. I hadn't had this much of his total attention in ages. It was too nice of a feeling to spoil.

"It's nothing serious. Speaking with Topher later about taking time off will suck, royally. He's such a control freak douchebag. I'm also waiting on Liam to send over tonight's copy, which I'm sure will be chockful of changes I'll have to deal with five minutes before we go live. It's a never-ending string of bullshit drama, but being able to spend uninterrupted time with you will be well worth the torture. Sometimes I miss being a nobody beat reporter. It was easier. I enjoyed myself more. You're well versed in how it goes," I partially fibbed with a smile. There were many times I wished to return to my old network because there was far less politics and stress, and considerably more freedom.

"Well, Mrs. Winters. First and foremost, you are not, and never have been, a nobody. However, it appears you're in a state of deep distress. As your personal therapist, I strongly encourage you to follow physician's orders, allowing me full ability to use questionable techniques to shake the station from your mind," he growled playfully, diving under the covers.

The moment, a perfect way to start any random day, was interrupted by the sound of Nick's phone ringing.

"Ignore it. The doctor is out and doesn't give a damn about anything that's not in this bed," he said, not coming up for air. I would've let things go if it wasn't for my cell joining in the party.

"Hold on a second, Nick. This could be important," I replied, scanning the new text from Liam Stevens, my producer. I could only imagine what I looked like, because I felt every ounce of color drain from my face as I read the words. A hot, creepy, prickling sensation crept up my spine, settling at the base of my neck.

"What's going on? What is it? Everything okay?" Nick slid his back up against the headboard, reached for his reading glasses, then took the device from my hand. "Oh, you've got to be shitting me," he hissed.

"Read the entire article, please, so we can get it over with in one fell swoop," I requested as my fingertips aggressively rubbed my temples. I stopped skimming the piece – if one could even consider what was written that – immediately after appraising the headline. A headache and heartburn slammed together in an instant.

"Divorce rumors surrounding self-help author and

podcaster Doctor Nicholas Winters and his wife, Jillian Winters, host of *The Bottom Line*, were confirmed yesterday as the two were spotted entering the law office of celebrity attorney, Charles Downey, separately. Insiders say the two have been at war for months because of Mrs. Winters', who's been dubbed 'a winter that never thaws,' infidelity, explosive personality, money hungry ways, and deep-rooted desires to do whatever necessary to remain in the spotlight. The two went in, but weren't seen exiting. Calls to their representatives have gone unanswered, but our insiders suggest the two are definitely done," Nick read. "There's more, but you've got the gist."

"Oh my God."

"Okay, okay. Deep breath, babe. It's a rag paper. Yes, people read them, but the validity of their reporting is almost always called into question. As for whom their insiders are? I have no idea – it doesn't matter anyway. If we find out, what's the plan? We attack them? No. Come on now. You and I've been quiet about our lives to friends and family. It's also highly doubtful that anyone in the law office yesterday said anything to the fake press. Chances are there is nobody leaking information – just some scumbag reporter who followed us and snapped a few crappy pictures. This will blow over. We have people who we pay a lot of money to handle things like this. Let's get up and dressed. I'll call Nate. You reach out to Jack. They'll tell us what our next move should be," Nick said calmly.

Getting off the bed, I headed to the walk-in closet, grabbing at the first matching outfit I could find.

"These assholes are going to destroy my marriage *and* career," I mumbled angrily.

Approaching me from the left, Nick took firm hold of my shoulders. "Look at me. Focus on only me. Screw the world out there. It's just us, here, in this room, together. Let go of the control you're trying to hold onto because we both know there's nothing to grab hold of. This is out of our hands. It's part of the life we live. Something we were aware of when we signed up to become celebrities. There will always be lies, stories, and rumors. It's all white noise. As long as we know the truth and remain steadfast with our priorities, we're good. Trust my lead, Jill. No one is going to ruin our lives, unless we let them. Don't fight me," he said as he tilted my chin upwards. Once eye contact was established, he continued.

"Inhale, slowly through the nose." Softly, he counted to four. "Hold it." Another four second count. "Exhale from the mouth with a sigh." We did this a handful of times before my body unclenched. It didn't matter how often Nick assisted me in the calming down process, because there was always a certain level of awestruck over his talents. He could quiet the roughest seas in the matter of seconds. "All better?"

"For the moment," I replied, knowing damn good and well the panic would return. *When,* was the question.

"That's my girl. Go take a hot shower. That will help relax you further. We've gone through this before. It will be all right. As for your show and ratings, stop worrying. You have the number one news program on air. Even if people hate and are judging you, they're still tuning in every night, and will continue to do so because you're an incredible, insightful, fair, and honest anchor," Nick soothed while he put on a pair of dark gray slacks and a sage green, fitted, V-neck sweater before exiting the bedroom.

Truth was, we had endured quite a bit of tabloid speculation over the years, but to have to deal with this crap hot on the heels of attempting to work on our marriage seemed potentially damaging. I wasn't stupid. Armed with the knowledge last night's lustful roll in the hay was what one might refer to as a "honeymoon phase," the house of cards, held together by cheap glue, placed on a foundation of quicksand could fall at any point, *but* Nick made a strong point. We both employed people to put fires like this out. Anecdotes, fabrications, and buzzes went with the territory. Plus, he didn't appear too terribly upset by the article. Why should I?

While I shampooed my hair, my thoughts wandered back and forth from Nick to the current media shit show. Things with Nick had been rather fairytale-like, even during dark times, and even with his family despising me. He'd always been my rock, my beacon of light, and port in any storm. Shortly after we married, my parents passed away in a horrific car accident. With no brothers or sisters, I struggled with loneliness and abandonment issues. I clung to Nick, often begging him to promise he'd never leave me. As a therapist, I suppose he understood, because each mini breakdown I suffered was greeted with strong, loving, compassionate arms and words. Without him by my side, I doubt I'd have ever been able to move past the tragedy.

As for the Winters family, the moment they laid eyes on me they wanted me gone. Condescending tones, hushed whispers upon entering rooms, side eye looks, and passive aggressive statements were the cornerstone of my relationship with all of them, except for his grandparents. I'd never be one hundred percent sure if they cared for me or not, but if they didn't, they never showed it. The only time I came in handy for Tag and Miranda was when they'd want me to pull strings at the station so one of them could push their political agenda live on air – which I never did. It wasn't my job to broker interviews. Quite frankly, I never fully understood how Nick fit in with the lot. Of course they shared physical resemblances, but personality wise – night and day.

Even after I obtained my current position hosting my own primetime news show, the Winters still thought little of me, often stating I was only offered the gig because of my married surname. That assumption was the farthest thing from the truth. In fact, I wanted to use my maiden name of Locke instead, but Topher Robbins, the station owner, insisted I didn't. Yes, luck and Nick played a large role in my career, but aside from a quick introduction to Liam Stevens by Nick at a launch party for one of Nick's books, I did the rest.

Because I'm a Winters, viewers expected me to side with Nick's family and their party affiliation, but that's not how I operate. Right or wrong, I deliver information to the public free from bias. If that meant ruffling feathers, so be it. It wasn't my place to change my viewer's minds. It is my job to inform, to uncover all aspects of a story, then convey the findings to whoever tuned in. They could put the pieces together and form their own opinions. However my audience utilized that information was on them – free will. Being so many networks held strong allegiances to specific sides, my take and style quickly earned the station the highest ratings they'd ever seen, but in order to keep the pace I was going at, other aspects of my life had to take the backseat – for one, Nick. He'd done the same with his career as well, but I couldn't control that. I could only take responsibility for me and my actions. Tonight, I'd do the show, then put in for immediate time off. In all the years I'd been there I never missed work, even when I was as sick as a dog. I'd powered through migraines, the stomach flu, common colds, and so on all without compromising my quality of performance. If they said no, I'd pitch a fit and threaten to quit. Besides, Liam and my assistant, Lyla Marx, could use a vacation as well.

Reaching for the house phone after dressing, I called my manager, Jack Ramsey.

"I know. I know, Jill. I saw the article. Slime balls from all of the tabloids have been calling nonstop since four in the morning sniffing around for a comment. I just got off the phone with Nate. He's in the same boat. All I need to know is are you divorcing or not?" Jack said the second he answered.

"We're not," I replied, unsure of how to spin why we were at Charles' office in the first place without giving away too much personal information. To date, we succeeded in keeping our marital troubles quiet.

"Might I ask why you two were visiting Mr. Downey yesterday? It makes sense based on recent rumors. You and Nick have been spotted arguing. You're barely on speaking terms, and haven't attended an event together in years," he pressed.

"Look, Nick and I hit a rough patch. We're fine now. For my sanity, please spin this the same way you've spun the adultery rumors." My tone was short.

"You got it. In the meantime, go out with Nick in public today. Show a united front – that all is well. Hold hands, kiss, skip through Central Park for all I care – just be seen outside, happy, and in love. I'll have Maryann send over a copy of the joint statement Nate and I will draft this afternoon."

"Thanks for handling this."

"That's my job. If the station gives you hell over this, give me a shout. I'll call that crap weasel Robbins myself," Jack said, then hung up.

Damn it! The frigging station and Topher.

The second Robbins caught wind of this he'd explode. In the past, we'd had several run-ins over news stories I'd been the central focus of. Each time, the PR department, along with Jack, carefully crafted ways to turn negatives into positives. Usually, I'd read something management prepared on air first thing, then everyone would pretend nothing happened. Our focus remained on the heart and soul of the show, which I didn't mind at all.

"See?" Nick smiled brightly. He stood in the doorframe of the bedroom. His arms were loosely crossed against his broad chest. "All taken care of. Rearview mirror material. Now, onto better, cheerier, more fun things. I know you've got a show tonight, but after, when you get home, I may have a surprise or two up my sleeve. Nate and Jack want us to be seen out and about around town, but I say screw it. I want you all to myself. We can do the photo op tomorrow." Mischief danced in those vibrant green eyes of his.

A grin braced my lips. Nick had that ability. He knew how to break me, pull me from the wreckage, make me forget the world around us was on fire. Right then and there I was one hundred percent sure I was all in. I wanted him, us, this.

"Is that a smile I see?" Nick teased.

"Maybe. Don't get too full of yourself. Breakfast?" I raised an eyebrow.

"Nah, babe. I've got other things in mind for now," he growled, throwing me over his shoulder and onto the bed. "Getting up and dressed was one of my worst ideas to date."

With a giggle, I gave into his will, falling victim to false hope.

Chapter 3

Jillian

Begrudgingly, I left Nick home to go to work. It had been sometime since I experienced missing him upon leaving. Truth be told, it kind of felt exhilarating. The marriage of annoyance and ache coupled with the excitement to return to his side proved powerful. The day had been, dare I say, perfect. We talked, but not about anything pressing. We caught up. I had no idea Nick had signed a three-book deal with a major publishing house, nor did I know his Podcast was getting ready to go global. The best part? Nick and I laughed – a lot. Real, genuine, honest laughter filled the once darkened hallways of our home.

After I exited my chauffeured Lincoln Town Car, a perk from the station, Lyla immediately greeted me at the station's back doors. Shedding my coat and purse, Lyla took possession of my items and followed me down the long, narrow corridor to my office. Her arms were filled with folders, while her fingers tightly clutched her cell phone.

"Senator Joshua Millburn canceled last minute. His replacement will be Judge Ethel Wasser. Currently, she's in hair and makeup. The Judge is amenable to any and all discussions as long as they have nothing to do with her personal life, which loosely translates to, stay away from mentioning her alcoholic son who's in rehab, again. Anything involving politics or current events is up for grabs. I know its short notice, but Liam made a list of topics for you to touch upon; mostly women in government and the roles they play. If it were me, I'd focus on her recent decision regarding the Babette King murder trial, and the rumors she's being considered for the open Supreme Court Justice chair, but those are just my simple suggestions. Everything is on your desk along with a few other things that require your signature. Also, Mr. Robbins wants to speak with you after the show. He left strict instructions for you to meet him in his office and to bring Liam with you," Lyla informed.

"I'm not shocked Millburn bailed. I had a feeling he would after yesterday's news explosion. His PR guys are probably working overtime trying to find a PC way to spin why he was in a cheap motel room with a bunch of underage hookers as the FBI raided the dump. I've got a few things I'd like to chat about with the Judge, but I'm liking your suggestions. Excellent work. Thank you. As for Topher – tell him to kiss my ass," I replied, shuffling papers around my messy work surface.

Lyla's expression was priceless. She wasn't sure how to respond to my Topher comment.

"Relax. I was joking. Tell the little shit I'll be there the second my mic is unplugged."

A nervous laugh came from Lyla's mouth. "I'll get right on that," she answered, before taking her leave.

I liked Lyla, quite a bit actually. She reminded me a lot of myself when I was her age – ambitious. What made her stand out was she didn't want to be a gofer forever. Lyla had expressed hopes and dreams of one day having her own primetime show, so introductions to all the right people were made whenever possible. Her thoughts, ideas, and opinions were always encouraged and fully supported. Other on-air talent at the network didn't allow their assistants as much free rein as I'd given Lyla, which I never understood why. Egos, perhaps. Eventually, someone in the industry would notice Lyla's talent. The thought of losing her sucked, but watching her succeed would feel far better.

Glancing at the desk clock, I spoke to myself. "In five, four, three, two…hello, Liam." I didn't have to look up to know my predictable, amazing, gifted producer Liam Stevens had entered the room.

"You're killing me, Jill. You know that, right? A slow, painful bleed out." He huffed, closing the door, then taking a seat on the white leather sofa. Reaching into his laptop bag, he produced four antacid tablets. Popping them into his mouth, he sighed, heavily.

"Jack and Nate have the whole tabloid nonsense under control," I said, still digging through a never-ending mountain of papers. The more I shuffled them, the bigger the stack grew.

"I'm sure everyone has a firm handle on this, *but* I hate to burst your bubble. Robbins is fuming. Did Lyla tell you he wants to meet with both of us post-show?"

"Yes. I'm not worried about it. Topher isn't going to do a damn thing. He'll huff and puff like he always does, but nothing will come of it. That jackass needs us more than we need all of this. Without our show, no one would watch this station."

"Jill, we're *all* replaceable in this industry. Don't think you're untouchable. Here today, gone tomorrow, without a backwards glimpse. I can't tell you how many times I've seen it happen. The next pretty face will quickly cover-up yours on ads and billboards. You better go in there sans the attitude. Leave the gigantic chip on your shoulder here, safely tucked away in this space. Anyway, what's going on with you and Nick? I'm aware you've been having marital problems, but I didn't realize you were headed for a divorce. I thought you'd scream and shout a bit, then work it out." Liam leaned back into the sofa, stretched, and closed his tired eyes.

"We've been 'separated' for some time now, but we're still living in the same house. A few months ago, *he* filed for divorce. *Not* me. Then, yesterday, while hammering out terms in my lawyer's office, I'm not sure what happened. Nick had a change of heart. He says he wants to work things out," I explained, plopping onto the chair across from him.

"Why didn't you say anything to me?" Liam's eyes opened, revealing a mix of genuine concern and upset.

"I don't know. Talking about it hurt. Plus, I wanted to keep it private."

"Kendra and I are always here for you, Jill. We may not be blood, but that doesn't matter. We love you *and* Nick very much. You're *not* alone."

Kendra, Liam's wife of forty years, quickly befriended me the second we met at one of Nick's book events. As we waited in line to use the restroom, she struck up a conversation about how exceptional of a therapist Nick was. Flattered by her kind words, I introduced them. The ironic part? Nick had been chatting with Liam about potentially doing a fill-in guest spot at the network. As Nick and Kendra spoke, I conversed with Liam about being a journalist for a local news network. After that night, I didn't hear or see from either of them until one random morning, months later, when

Liam emailed me asking to meet up for coffee. Just like that, I had an interview to host a nightly news show. A week later, it was mine. I owed everything to that chance happening, Nick's talent, and Liam Stevens.

"That means the world to me. It really does, but everything is fine. I promise," I assured.

"Don't shut me out again, Jill. If you don't want to talk about whatever with me, call Kendra. She'll always lend you a shoulder to cry on."

"I'm sorry. I won't." I paused, smiling warmly at Liam's loving nature. I tilted forward, reached for, and briefly squeezed his hand. "Listen, after Topher bitches me out over whatever crawled up his ass and died today, I'm going to request a brief sabbatical. Nick and I want to take a quick vacation, get away from everything to reconnect. If we stand any chance of making our marriage work, we've got to do it in a drama and distraction free environment. Around here, that's an impossible feat. Don't even attempt to pretend otherwise, because we both know it."

"I see that appeal going over like a fart in an elevator. Topher won't go for it. Especially not with the CAT Network only a few points behind us in the rating polls these past few months. You're the big-ticket item around here. If you're out, the ship will sink – and fast. Don't *you* even attempt to pretend otherwise."

"I'm aware, which is why I need you to help me come up with a rock-solid proposal for who will fill in while I'm away. I wouldn't ask if it wasn't absolutely necessary. Please, Liam?"

"I'll see what celebrities I can line up." He hesitated, pondering something in his head before continuing. "I don't talk about this often, but roughly fifteen years into my marriage, Kendra and I hit the skids, bad. I thought it was over for sure. All we ever did was yell and scream. We didn't see eye to eye on anything, ever. One evening, after a huge fight, she kicked me out. The kids were little. They had no idea what was going on. To this day they thought their father was away working. We were separated for about six months. I moved in with my older brother, Randy, you know, the retired detective. Worst time of my life. Anyway, my oldest fell off his bike – broke his arm. Kendra called from the hospital crying and scared. I ran to the ER like a bat out of hell. My kid was hurt. My wife was upset and worried. They needed me. A few hours later, when I was dropping them back home, she invited me in, and we talked – really talked, something we hadn't done for a while. It wasn't fun at all, but once we dug through all the hurt feelings, we came out on the other side just fine. Look at us now. Three grown, married, successful children, with twin grandbabies on the way.

"If you and Nick truly love each other, this bump in the road will be a story you'll tell one of your kids one day. Jill, and don't take this the wrong way, you've got to rein it in a bit. He's got a lot of work to do too, but your biggest problem is you haven't forgiven him for the Kelly incident." He stopped speaking momentarily, putting his hand up to halt any interjections. "Don't cheapen our relationship by lying and saying you're fine with what happened, because we both know you're not. You'll never be okay until you let it go. You haven't been the same since it happened. Every single aspect of you changed. You're worth more than the heaping bag of crud you've been dragging around. Just some food for thought. All right, I need you in hair and makeup. Show starts in a half hour."

"That's why I love you most and best. Thank you," I said, standing, leaning over, and kissing the top of his bald head.

"Yeah, yeah. What are producers who double as adopted dads for? Get your ass in gear, kiddo. We've got a job to do," he said and exited.

****

"I'm Jillian Winters, and that's the bottom line. Goodnight." My body remained frozen with a smile glued to my face, while my eyes were fixed on camera two waiting for Liam's cue.

"And, we're out. Great show, everyone. Another masterpiece for the books. Thank you for all of your talent, support, time, and help," Liam said, removing his headphones, and running both hands over his face. "Whenever you're ready, Jill."

Placing my mic pack on the desk, I let my shoulders slump. Having to maintain perfect posture for three consecutive hours took a toll on my back. Add the stress of having to deal with Topher and his arrogant belligerence on top of that, it was a miracle I could stand in the upright position at all.

"Let's get this over with," I said to Liam as we walked to the elevator bank.

In silence, we entered Topher's massive office space. You'd think being he was worth millions of dollars the area would've been decorated with taste and class, but no. The theme of his surroundings could best be described as "shabby cheap." Random stock art hung from the stark white walls. Worn, brown, Berber Carpet drew the eye away from the many hideous, dusty, plastic plants which were used to hide scuffs along the baseboards. Every detail down to the chairs screamed bargain basement, discount junk. Tension laced with anxiety caused my right leg to bounce up and down. The motion was greeted by Liam's hand holding the limb in place. Though he didn't speak a word, his head remained down inspecting his tablet. In his own way he was attempting to sooth me.

"Mrs. Winters. Mr. Stevens. Mr. Robbins will see you now," Topher's secretary informed us.

"Thank you, Janette," Liam replied, taking hold of my arm. "You are a strong, confident, badass woman. Pull it together," he whispered in my ear.

"I'm fine." I lied.

"Great. Tell your face that."

The reminder of who I was comforted me, but not enough to keep my stomach from turning. Upon entering Topher's private space, he gestured for us to sit, while he barked orders into the phone. After a few seconds, he slammed the receiver down on the cradle and looked up.

"Mr. Robbins," I began, but I was cut off mid-thought.

"I don't care what you have to say, Ms. Winters. Yesterday was going decently until *you* and *your* husband decided to ruin that for me. Again, with the damn tabloids. First, it was the affairs. Then, it was the diva-like behaviors. After that, it was the drunken fighting to the death with your husband in public, and let's not forget the verbal scuffle you got into with a fan. And, my two personal favorites – the mic mishap, and all of the off color, snide remarks you made during the Martin Waters interview. He's the goddamn Chief Medical Advisor for the President of the United States, but somehow you turned his medical advice into a personal narrative over how politicians are in bed with big pharma. Now, it's sneaking into a divorce lawyer's office. The shocking part is this is just from the past year alone. It doesn't account for the other shit you've put me through over the course of your employment at this network," Topher ranted.

"The interview wasn't my fault. My comments were taken out of context and spliced to suit the negative needs of other networks and the media in general. As for the *fighting to the death* argument with Nick, it never happened. A rag reporter made it up," I defended, because it was the truth. I'd been asked to conduct an interview with Martin Waters about an executive order a governor had given based off his professional suggestions. My words were chopped to pieces, then put back together via massive editing. The results portrayed me as an ignorant, uneducated, aggressive asshole. Jack was able to get his hands on the original recording and leaked that to the press, which instantly discredited my competitors. Case closed. The Nick argument story came out of left field. Plain and simple – it never went down. We'd have to have been out in public together for something like that to occur.

"I don't give a tiny rat's behind whose fault any of this is, because it becomes my problem regardless. This station has paid more in legal fees for you than any other person on staff. Get your house in order or else there's the damn door. Use it. Don't let it hit you on the ass on your way out. The only reason you haven't been let go, *yet*, is because of your ratings, which you're only a small part of creating. The man sitting beside you is responsible for making all the magic happen. Thank him you're not back at that shit station you used to work for, because if I had my way you would've been gone a long time ago. Oh, and while we're at it, put a lock on your husband's mouth. He's become the king of too much information. It's as if someone shoots him with a sodium pentothal dart in the neck before he gives any kind of interview. He keeps flapping his gums like a whiny, snowflake liberal, pushing his agenda. We get the backlash of it here. Do you understand me, Ms. Winters? Enough already. Damn it."

In that moment Topher resembled the product of a one-night stand between a rat and a weasel. His thin frame, pointy face, and sharp features made him one of the most unattractive men I've ever laid eyes on. His wife – a total knockout. The young, tall, leggy, blonde married him solely for money. That was obvious to anyone who'd seen them interact at company parties. I couldn't help but stare at his ash brown hair for a hot second. It was always so perfectly styled and never moved. Often Liam and I debated if it was a toupee or not. My vote was always toupee.

"I do, and have a request of my own." I forced a tiny smile.

"What?" he snapped.

"I'd like some time off for personal reasons, starting as soon as possible." I held my breath waiting for him to explode.

"Best idea you've ever had, Ms. Winters. Mr. Stevens, I assume you've got guest hosts lined up?"

"I'm working on that now. I'll be here in Jillian's absence to make sure the show continues on as is. I'm thinking left wing verses right wing co-hosts – watch the conversations heat up. No Hollywood celebrities. Cheapens our format and credibility. I know a few senators, congress people, and judges whom might like an opportunity to sit in for Jillian. If you have any suggestions about what you'd like to see while she's away, my door is always open, sir," Liam replied.

The air I'd been holding in finally released its strangling grip over my bones. Relief washed over every ounce of my body almost immediately. My muscles instantly unclenched. The churning acid inside of my stomach calmed, allowing my heart rate and blood pressure to return to normal levels. The combination of everything cooled my core temperature, extinguishing the raging fire from within. All that was left was to get the hell out of Satan's office.

"I have a few ideas, but we can discuss them later. I'll call you. The wife and I are meeting friends for dinner in a half hour," Topher said. His tone and overall body language was considerably friendlier with Liam than me. "How much time do you want?" he asked, turning his neck in my general direction.

"At least three months. Possibly longer, but I fully plan on returning," I answered.

"Fine. When you decide you're ready to rejoin the team, you'll have no more chances. No more strikes. One more fuck up and you're done. You'll find yourself standing on the unemployment line. Do I make myself clear?"

"Crystal," I responded, rising.

Liam shook Topher's slimy, slim, girl-like hand. The two exchanged closing pleasantries before we left. I, on the other hand, remained silent. If another word had to spawn from my mouth it would've been a bad one. After a hasty goodbye to Liam, I raced out of the back door and straight into the Lincoln Town Car. Once the driver cleared the block, I reached for my phone. I had to call Nick to share the good news.

"This is Nick. Leave a message," his voicemail said.

"Hey. It's me. I'm on my way home. Can't wait to see you," I recorded, then hung up. By the time I got to the main gates, Nick had yet to return my call. The three texts I sent went unanswered as well. The house was pitch black. Nick's Lexus SUV was gone. Deactivating the alarm, something within me urged to proceed with an abundance of caution. Why? I don't know, but Nick was a constant communicator. Even when busy with work, even when we were at each other's throats, he'd always find a second to reply. A funny feeling sat in the pit of my stomach.

"Raul, when did Doctor Winters leave?" I asked, buzzing the security booth at the apron of the driveway. The main reason Nick's parents purchased this particular house for us was for its security features. Other reasons included, but were certainly not limited to, bragging rights, and them showboating their money and ability to afford luxury items, whereas my family could not.

"Doctor Winters left about an hour after you went to the station, Mrs. Winters," Raul said.

"Did he say where he was going, or when he'd be back?"

"No, ma'am."

"Did he take off in a hurry?"

"Not any faster than usual. He approached the gates, waved, then took off west. Is something the matter? Should I call the police?"

"That won't be necessary."

"I have security stationed in their usual positions. No one has been in or out since Doctor Winters exited the premises. Is there anything else I can assist with?"

"No. Thank you." The knot in my gut grew tighter.

Taking the stairs two by two, I ran to our bedroom, throwing the closet door open. His clothing remained neatly hung, same with the dresser drawers. The guestroom wardrobe was untouched as well, but Nick had a lot of clothing. I frantically checked the attic for missing luggage, but all twelve pieces sat in the corner. Rushing back down to the first floor, I found my personal laptop on the kitchen counter. Impatiently waiting for it to load, I searched every surrounding room. The stove had empty pots on three burners, and several pantry ingredients sat on the center island beside two large mixing bowls. Inside the formal dining room, the table had been partially set. It appeared Nick was planning on cooking dinner and possibly ran out to grab groceries? But it doesn't take nearly five hours to shop for food. Even if he was preparing a banquet it still wouldn't render that long to collect provisions.

My thoughts raced to Nick being in an accident. Car accidents were an Achilles' heel. Something which caused me powerfully consuming anxiety whenever Nick was late or took too long to answer a call. My brain automatically played out such horrific scenarios that I couldn't function until I heard his voice. Nick knew this. He'd never leave me hanging. For him not to even send an "I'm okay," message proved nerve-wracking.

Once the computer loaded, I attempted to track Nick's phone, but failed. It had been shut off. The last ping glowed around the St. Luke's Roman Catholic Church parking area. It wasn't too far from the house, but a place neither of us visited unless absolutely necessary. We weren't religious people. That didn't mean we didn't have faith or shared beliefs, but attending mass wasn't something we did – ever. Not even on Christmas or Easter. Why Nick was there confused me.

Because stress is a powerful force, I decided to take a quick ride by the building. Nick wasn't exactly the handiest man alive, so I calmed my raging thoughts by rationalizing that if he'd gotten a flat tire or had a fender bender, he might still be there. His phone being off was more than likely the result of a dead battery. It wouldn't be the first time Nick allowed that to happen by day's end. Without me or his assistant reminding him late afternoon to charge the device, often it ran out of juice having him resort to using one of our phones.

Being the late hour, few cars were on the road. Thankfully, traffic lights worked in my favor. The lot was huge, but empty, all except for one large, black Lexus. Pulling up next to his SUV, I peered inside of it. The vehicle was empty. Getting out of my car, I conducted a fairly detailed visual inspection. No major scratches or dents were seen, but under the dim glow of the streetlights, it was difficult to accurately assess any minor damage. Tugging the driver's side door handle, it refused to budge. I peeked through the window. Everything appeared normal. Reaching for my cell, I tried Nick again. No answer.

"This is Nick. Leave a message."

"Nick, it's me. I'm standing by your car in the parking lot of St. Luke's. Where are you? Could you call me back, please? I'm starting to freak out."

I waited for roughly two hours in my car for him to call or show up, but he didn't. Around two in the morning a police cruiser rolled up. The cop got out and approached the scene.

"Is everything okay, ma'am?" A young beat officer inquired.

"Yes. No. I don't know," I said, desperately trying to remain calm.

"Would you mind stepping out of your vehicle?"

I did.

"What's going on?" he asked.

"This is my husband's SUV. When I got home from work he wasn't there, so I tracked his phone here. This is the last place it says he was before his phone shut off. I drove here and now I'm waiting for him to come back," I explained.

"I understand you're concerned, but this is a private parking lot. You can't be here."

"I have to find Nick." My patience was wearing thin as my nerves rose to the surface. A frightful "dead in a ditch" scenario began playing on a loop inside of my mind.

"Again, I understand, but you have to vacate the lot, or I'm going to have to arrest you for trespassing."

"My husband is missing, Officer..." I said, squinting at his name tag.

"Bachman. Have you been drinking or taking any narcotics tonight, ma'am?"

"No." I felt my expression sour.

"Would you mind participating in a field sobriety test?"

"I'm not drunk nor high. I'm stone cold sober, but if blowing into your little machine and jumping up and down while reciting the alphabet backwards means you'll find my husband, then fine. Let's get this over with."

Twenty minutes later, and only after he ran my and

Nick's license plates, thoroughly examining my identification, registration, and insurance card, Officer Idiot confirmed I was in sound mind and not some drugged out psycho lunatic.

"Listen, Mrs. Winters. Your husband is a grown man. He's not an at-risk adult or a child. Sometimes people take off. If he's not back in forty-eight hours, call the station and they'll file a missing person report," the cop offered, dismissively.

"You don't think it's odd his SUV is here, unattended? It's not strange when I left the house he said he'd be home when I returned? It doesn't raise a red flag his phone is off while all this is going on?" I challenged.

"He hasn't been missing for forty-eight hours, and nothing about his vehicle looks suspicious. Wherever he is, he's fine."

"Do you understand my husband is a celebrity? He's famous. Millions of people not only here in the US, but all over the world know his name. Mine too, for that matter." This moron was beginning to piss me off. How lazy and uncaring could one human being be? Wasn't it his job to serve and protect the citizens of his community? Didn't my over inflated tax dollars fund his salary, pension, and benefits?

"Celebrity or not, we treat everyone the same. Has anyone threatened him or you recently? Has anyone called or reached out for money? Any blackmail requests?"

"Well, no – not that I'm aware of."

"Then wait the mandatory forty-eight hours, ma'am. You're going to need to leave this lot immediately. If your husband doesn't move his vehicle by this afternoon, I'm going to have it towed. Go home. He'll be fine. Have a good night." Before I had a chance to protest, he was in his cruiser and backing up.

You frigging lazy piece of crap. You better hope he's fine because if he's not I swear to everything bright and beautiful I will make it rain black rain in your world until the day you die.

Snapping a few quick pictures of Nick's Lexus and the surrounding area, I returned to my car, and headed home. It wasn't shocking Nick wasn't there upon my arrival. I didn't expect him to be because the churning in my gut knew something was amiss. What? I hadn't a clue, but I'd get to the bottom of it.

Chapter 4

Nick

The second Jillian left the house, I immediately went to work. Tonight had to be perfect. Pretty much every night for the foreseeable future had to go smoothly to make sure our marriage survived. Her center had thawed a bit, but a watchful guard remained firmly in place. It was my job to get her to put the shield down. Considering we hadn't slept together in months, last night's and this morning's intimacies were fantastic. She was present, unlike in the past where her mind was elsewhere. After my affair, all closeness died. Justifiably so. From that point forward, she'd lie on her back with her head turned, her eyes tightly closed, and her hands down by her side. She refused to fully undress, leaving her bra and shirt on. When the deed was complete, she'd hop off the bed like she was on fire, and run to the shower without saying a word. The few times I attempted to remove her top, keep her beside me, or switch things up, she'd stop the entire act faster than it began.

I'd counseled many people and couples over the years who endured similar hardships, but choices had to be made – you stayed or you left. Simple enough. Jillian chose to remain married, which meant she had only one option – let the indiscretion go, which she couldn't and didn't, often freezing me out, or doling out passive aggressive punishments such as embarking upon her own extramarital affairs. Due to immense guilt, I allowed her to act however she felt on any given day without repercussions, until her hostile behaviors became too much to handle. As a therapist, that was wrong. As a husband, I was torn. However, I never gave Jillian reason to believe I'd ever cheat again, but some indiscretions, no matter how hard we attempt to erase them, by no means vanish. The memory, the anguish, remains permanently seared inside of our souls, never relenting.

Armed with a shopping list and about a dozen places to hit up before she returned, I took off. The plan was to recreate the first time we shared a private meal together. Granted, it was a long time ago, and quite possibly she wouldn't remember, but I did. I was living off campus in my own small apartment. We'd been going out for a handful of months, and I was determined that would be the night we'd sleep together for the first time. Whenever we'd go beyond heavy petting, she'd slam on the brakes, suggesting she wasn't ready, that she wanted to make sure the relationship was solid and going somewhere before we shared strong connecting intimacies. Jillian was afraid of creating a temporary emotional attachment, which when broken, would hurt her tremendously. As an educated adult today, I fully understand her needs back then, but as a horny guy in his early twenties, I just wanted to get in her pants. She was hot, mysterious, brilliant, adventurous, fearless, and level-headed, yet loving and soft at the same time. Though not a good cook by any stretch of the imagination, I was confident if I was able to pull off Chicken Marsala, roasted potatoes, grilled asparagus, and a tossed salad once, I could certainly do it again.

Passing the security booth, I waved at Raul and Jon. Initially, I wasn't a fan of the armed guard theme of the property, but as the years drew on, it grew on me. Even though I was the "anti-everything Winters" spokesperson for the family, I did enjoy the finer things in life. It made me feel superior to others, a trait I wasn't fond of, but a part of my being I couldn't shed. Truthfully? Didn't want to. I allowed myself private pleasures such as accepting the house from my parents – though it had been put in Jillian's name so the sensation of me being tethered to them wasn't felt, weekly massages, spa treatments, manicures, designer clothing, expensive cars, lavish vacations, and so on, but I never allowed myself to be seen that way in public. While giving interviews or attending fan events, I'd always make sure to wear clothing similar to theirs. If Jillian was in attendance, I'd request the same of her. In order to be relatable, to sell books, to have people listen to the podcast, they had to feel we were one and the same. If they wore box store jeans and I had on the identical brand, they'd be more open to my message, deeming me someone who was down to Earth. Not a stuck-up douchebag who was only in it for the cash.

Yes, the money, fame, and popularity were all completely amazing, but I truly did and do want to help individuals live their best lives. With extensive knowledge and a unique approach to various alternative psychological treatments, I've assisted many people. You have no idea how fulfilling that is. And sure, one could make a strong case I was a fraud using mind tricks for personal gain, often I'd find myself playing that game during quiet moments, but I worked hard, long hours, and made copious sacrifices. Why shouldn't I be allowed to enjoy the toils of my labor?

Jillian's favorite florist was my first stop. The night of our initial intimate encounter I'd purchased Lilies of the Valley. I strategically placed two dozen scented candles around my apartment. The small glass table was set with a navy-blue tablecloth and silver napkins – which incidentally ended up being the color scheme for our wedding. Once we found our footing, I'd suggest renewing our vows, but that was an idea to toy with later. Combining a chilled bottle of Dom Perignon, smooth jazz on the stereo, and dimmed lights, an ambiance of romance instantly materialized. The meal finished with imported French macarons. Our evening was perfect. We made love several times, and she stayed until the morning. From that point forward, we were inseparable. A year later, I proposed. A year after that, we were married. It was as if that one date got the ball rolling. Trust and intimacy had slammed together. Perhaps the same would occur again, proving lightning can strike the same area twice.

Feeling particularly hopeful, my smile faded the moment my cell rang and the car speakers alerted who was calling.

"Call from Tag Winters," the virtual assistant announced. A chill shot up my spine upon hearing the name. Knowing it was better to deal with him now rather than later, I replied to the automated voice.

"Connect." After a brief pause, I spoke again. "Hello, Dad. How are you and Mom?"

"We're fine. Doing great. What the hell is going on with you and *that wife* of yours? Did you finally wake up and decide to dump her?" My father's tone and delivery was hard and rude as always.

"Jillian, *my wife*, and I are well. Based off your comment, I'm assuming you saw the tabloid article. We're not splitting up. Sorry to disappoint you. We had an appointment with our lawyers to address contract negotiation issues," I lied, making sure to remain calm, inhaling and exhaling meaningfully. This technique helped me to navigate many stressful situations over the years.

"One day you'll realize she's beneath you. Totally undeserving of the Winters name. Whenever you're ready, call Ally Newman. She's a beast. You'll end up with everything. By the time Ally's done ripping into your ex, she'll be homeless on the streets."

"Anything new going on? How are Grandpa and Grandma feeling?" I asked, changing the subject because all of the mindful breathing in the world wouldn't stop me from wanting to reach through the receiver and strangle him.

"My parents are fine. They'll outlive us all. Your mother has been busy helping Keira build an appropriate 'wife of a presidential hopeful' wardrobe. Your brother, let me tell you. That kid has a good, strong chance at winning the party nomination. We'll be vacationing with them, your sisters, and their families next week in Martha's Vineyard. Got to strategize. I'm beyond proud of Jackson and my girls. Creating laws, pushing agendas, passing bills – real chips off the old block," he said, passive aggressively gushing.

"Guess Jillian and my invitation got lost in the mail, *again*." Two could play at the go-screw-yourself game.

"You're always busy – touring, interviews, and she's got that little show she hosts. We assumed you wouldn't be available," Tag replied dismissively.

"You know what happens when you assume, right, Dad?" I paused. "And, for the record, Jillian's show isn't *little*. It's actually the top watched and highest rated news program currently on the air."

"What are you doing to promote Jackson?" The man was a master sidestepper. A true politician.

"I can't do that. As a therapist, influencer, and someone who disagrees with Jackson's platform, I cannot endorse him."

"What's to disagree with?" My father was dancing on the fine line between feigning cordialness and shouting.

"I don't want to argue, Dad. Jackson lives in this warped little bubble where he believes the world should operate like its nineteen thirty again. Women should be barefoot and pregnant in the kitchen. A man's only job should be to make a living, and everyone goes to church on Sunday. All homes should have an arsenal of weapons, and no woman's voice needs to be heard. I don't agree with that. I am a firm believer, as humans walking this Earth, we all have free will, and because of that, we are allowed to make choices as we see fit. A man holds no more importance than a woman. Regardless of gender, race, sexual orientation, religion, creed, and so on, we are, and always will be, equals."

"What about Jillian? Being on her show would give him more exposure. It will also show family solidarity. Set that up." The man had actively ignored everything I'd just said.

"But only a few seconds ago she was, '*that wife of yours*,' who hosted a '*little*' show, and you were rooting for us to divorce. Plus, let's not forget about the family vacation she and I were conveniently not asked to attend.

No, Dad. First of all, much like myself, Jillian needs to remain neutral. Secondly, she doesn't control, nor does she have a say in whom the station books as guests. If Jackson wants an interview, he needs to have *his* people contact the network. Jillian and I don't play the nepotism game. If they want him on, they'll place him on a show she is not the host of to keep it fair. Lastly, even if the station allowed her to host, there's no way that segment would ever run smoothly. She and I share similar beliefs. If you ever had a conversation with her or watched the program, you'd know Jillian is a bar pusher who challenges all of her guests – even the ones she agrees with." My head shook involuntarily. This was exactly how every single one-to-one went down with him. He'd never change.

"Need I remind you, *family first*, Nicholas. Jackson is blood. Jillian is nothing," he said with a sharp snap in his tone.

"Duly noted. However, we're going to have to agree to disagree on this. I have to go. It was great speaking with you. Please send my warmest regards to everyone, and enjoy the upcoming family gathering." I had to hang up and fast. If the conversation lingered any longer, I'd lose my shit. I was a stone's throw away from saying things I'd regret as it stood.

By the time he said his longwinded, condescending goodbyes, I found my fingers wrapped so tightly around the steering wheel that my knuckles were white. Even my steady breathing turned shallow and hard. My shoulders had tensed to the point of producing burning neck pain.

"You stupid son of a bitch! Get off your damn phone and pay attention to what you're doing! The entire road isn't yours!" I raged at a young male motorist in an electric blue Jeep Wrangler who'd cut me off. Anger so deep, anger I worked endlessly to control broke free. The tiny sliver of rational thinking left inside of me urged I pull off the street to regain composure. I was better than this, and could control my inner rage. Glancing to the left, St. Luke's Roman Catholic Church came into focus. Never much of a religious person, I did, however, consider myself spiritual. Perhaps this was a sign of sorts. Turning into the nearly empty lot, I parked and entered the narthex. Something about the sanctuary caused instant relief. Aside from the fact the structure flourished with ornate architectural design, it offered something better than simple aesthetics – quiet and peace of mind. The warm incense laced air soothed and relaxed my stressed joints. When the large, wooden doors softly shut, sounds from the outside world ceased to exist. One could truly be alone with their thoughts, safe and protected in this building. Walking through the nave, I noticed a handful of older women seated up front praying the rosary. Selecting a pew closer to the back, I sat, unsure of what to do. Should I pray? Talk to God? Kneel? Make the sign of the cross?

"I usually just sit and think," a middle-aged, somewhat portly, nearly bald man spoke. His voice and presence initially startled me because I wasn't expecting it. He must've snuck in behind me being I hadn't seen him upon arriving. Totally unthreatening in appearance, he wore tan slacks, a green and white plaid, long-sleeve, button-down shirt, and brown leather boots. My composure returned to tranquil.

"Thanks. It's been a while since I've been to church," I said. I smiled, grateful for the man's input, but secretly wishing he'd leave me alone. The point of this exercise was to restore proper balance – figure out what the true trigger of my sudden outburst was. With him around, potentially chewing my ear off, that wouldn't occur.

"It's the one place the phrase, 'you can never go home again' doesn't apply."

"I suppose that's true. I'm Nick," I said, extending a hand. It became obvious this man wanted to speak and not sit quietly. As a therapist, on or off the clock, it was my job—however, right now it felt like more of an obligation—to help those in need.

"Warren," he answered, accepting the gesture and grinning warmly. "So, Nick, what brings you back to church?"

"Truthfully? I was speaking on the phone with someone who was pushing every button imaginable. I found myself in dire need of a break. St. Luke's was the first place I saw, so here I am." I had no idea why I admitted this to a stranger, but I did. People confessed a wide variety of things to me all the time. Why couldn't I be afforded the same right, especially when he was infringing on my private time?

"Sometimes we find ourselves confronted with others who are damaged souls. Because of that damage they cannot help themselves, and far too often they don't even realize their own internal issues. They don't understand the power of their words, actions, thoughts, and so on. Most times they're unaware of what they're doing. For them, it's just another status quo day. They truly believe they're mentally stable and healthy – that *you're* the one who needs counseling. No matter what you say or do they won't hear you or care about your needs. In these moments, Nick, we must have faith and remind ourselves these people aren't necessarily bad human beings, but rather ones who are acting from a place of wreckage and hurt. A wounded inner child is controlling them, not the adult exterior we're looking at while conversing. We must be mindful to view the masses as a whole, not only as a part. Once we understand them and their past, we can act accordingly while being aware of their behaviors. Their power is then weakened, and the hurt they're spewing doesn't bother us as much because we're aware of the roots," Warren explained. Quite honestly? His advice was exactly what I would've said to a patient experiencing a similar crisis. Add the uncertainty and anxiety over rebuilding with Jillian to the conversation from before with my father, and yeah, there was my perfect storm's explosion.

"Thank you, Warren. Even therapists need to be reminded of certain concepts every now and again. What you said helped," I said, looking him in the eyes.

"I apologize for asking this, but are you by chance Doctor Nicholas Winters? The famous psychotherapist who writes books and has the radio show?"

"I am, but I do not consider myself *famous* on any level." The volume of my voice lowered. At times, like now for example, I didn't wish for public attention. A case could be made that since I was a celebrity of sorts it was part of the package and I'd agree, but everyone deserved a little privacy as well. Jillian and I endured more than our fair share of personal invasions. Hell, we were currently in the middle of one.

"Oh dear. I've made you uncomfortable. Here you are seeking comfort and I'm outing you. It doesn't matter who you are. I'd never wish to make anyone feel ill at ease. We're all children of God. That's all we should place focus on."

"It's fine. No worries," I assured.

"You're too kind."

"I don't know if I'd go that far, but thank you. It was wonderful meeting you, Warren. The gentle reminder about human nature was much needed and tremendously appreciated. I best be going. Have a wonderful evening," I said, stood, and shook his hand again.

"Should you ever require any future help, you more than likely can find me right here." A warmness radiated throughout his entire being.

Exiting the doors, I made my way back to my SUV with a renewed sense of calm, faith, and balance. Running into Warren was a blessing of sorts. While smirking over how the Universe mysteriously worked, an excitement I hadn't experienced in a while danced inside of my soul. Screw what Tag and Miranda Winters thought. Jillian and I was the only thing that rendered my total energy and concentration.

"Hey, Nick," I heard Warren say from behind.

As I turned to face him, a sharp, bone rattling pain radiated throughout my core. Attempting to shake the discomfort proved useless. I fell to my knees while my hands held my ringing head.

"Easy does it. No need to panic. Just breathe," Warren said as he placed a white handkerchief over my mouth and nose.

Within mere seconds, my eyes felt heavy and my brain grew fuzzy. My lids opened and closed slowly until only one option remained. Sleep.

Chapter 5

Nick

Like a light switch turning on, my eyes flipped open. Consciousness greeted me with a throbbing head and a foggy mind. I found myself lying under a gauzy beige blanket on a somewhat soft twin-sized spring mattress. Slowly sitting, I steadied myself by taking a series of several deep breaths. My slacks and sweater had been replaced with thin cotton navy pajamas. Ivory slippers and a bathrobe were folded and placed neatly at the foot of the bed. Once my faculties appeared in tack, my focus shifted to the space. Six small rectangular basement-style windows illuminated the room. I was definitely under the main space of a home. Dark wood panels covered all four walls. The floor was carpeted in a harvest gold shag material throughout. Brass headboard beds were broken up by simple oak nightstands with avocado green gooseneck desk lamps atop. The sleeping setup neatly flanked three walls. The remaining partition was one long tan cabinet. Turning to the right, I opened the bottom nightstand drawer. The contents were stark white starched boxer shorts, crew neck undershirts, and tube socks. The top drawer held a black leather-bound Bible, a blue composition notebook, tissues, hand lotion, and two black ball-point pens.

This wasn't a hospital – that I was sure of, but

exactly what it was I hadn't a clue. What I did feel confident about was the man I'd met at the church – Warren, had something to do with this. Brief flashes of turning to face him in the parking lot came forward. He had to have struck me in the head because that's where the pain stemmed, and if I had to guess, I'd say he used chloroform on a rag to knock me out due to my current state of grogginess. But, why?

The whys don't matter. Getting the hell out of here does. Get up and get after it.

Shaking the haze and standing, three closed doors became my target. One of them had to lead to a staircase or possibly to the outside world. Tossing the blanket aside, careful steady steps lead to door number one – a closet housing a sea of heavily pressed ivory slacks, button down long and short sleeve shirts, knee-length skirts, and canvas slide on shoes. Glancing back, all of the beds housed the same pajamas I wore, precisely placed on each pillow. Turning my attention back to the day wear, my fingers inspected the material. Cotton, somewhat flimsy. The stitching was clearly home sewn. Shutting the pristinely organized wardrobe, my awareness turned to door number two – a bathroom. The area was nothing special and rather typical in fact – twin sinks, a vanity with a long rectangular mirror, a toilet, and a tub with a shower. Just like everything else, the room was white, clean, tidy, and systematized. The final door, door number three, was locked from the other side. That had to be the primary way out, but not the only means of escape. The windows were another option. It'd be a tight fit, but I could squeeze through. Where there's a will there's a way, right? Once on the other side, I'd figure out the rest. Baptism by fire – easy enough, I hoped. Approaching the closest one, the damn frame appeared bolted shut with exterior nails. Even with the back of a hammer the nails couldn't be removed because a heavy layer of glue held them in place. For a fleeting second, I contemplated using one of the lamps to smash the glass, but cracking triple pane windows would take many swings with a far sturdier object.

"Son of a bitch!" I hissed, turning to strike the adjacent wall.

"That's no way to behave, Brother Nicholas. We do not act out of anger or frustration here. This is a home of healing, love, comfort, and peace. However, I forgive you. In time I'm confident you'll learn our ways, eventually seeing the light," Warren said, standing to my right.

"What the hell is going on? Why did you attack, drug, and bring me here?" I shouted out of fear and anger – a lethal combination. It was fight or flight time, but my only option was fight, and damn it, I was ready for whatever this sick bastard had in mind.

"First, you must quiet yourself. Those in survival mode do not think, process, or function on an executive level. In order to comprehend your new life, you must be in a place of balance from within. Primal rage has no business in anyone's existence."

"Listen, Warren, or whoever the hell you really are, I don't want to be here which means you're holding me against my will. If you let me go right now, I won't press any charges." I attempted to rationalize with him, because it was as clear as the ruddy nose on his face, this man was a stark raving lunatic. If there's one thing in this world everyone should be made aware of its you cannot fight with crazy. You won't win.

"My name *is* Warren. Warren Lessor to be precise, but here you will call me Brother Warren. We're all brothers and sisters in this house. As for leaving, I'm sorry, but that isn't possible," he said coolly while taking a seat at the foot of one of the beds.

"You cannot hold me here, Warren. It's illegal. The criminal justice system refers to this type of situation as abduction and assault," I challenged, standing directly in front of him.

Taking a long, deep breath he spoke again. "You asked why I brought you here. The answer is simple – to save you."

"From what? My seven-figure salary? The mansion I live in? My admiring fans? My passion to help others? A career I adore? Yeah, my life is frigging terrible." Keeping my temper in check was a feat. The fuse within me had already been lit. I wasn't sure how long the wick would fizz before the inevitable explosion occurred.

"First, please refrain from cursing in this house. That kind of language will not be tolerated and has no place in any of our lives. It's vulgar, vile, and uncivilized. Secondly, I notice you mentioned material items and all of the riches one receives from fame. Not once did you mention your wife or family. Why is that?" he mused very matter-of-factly.

"Excuse me?"

"When we as humans sum up our lives, most mention spouses, children, and family first. You, on the other hand, did no such thing. Nicholas Winters went straight to what he perceives as his great fortune – wealth and all the trapping that go along with it. This tells me you may be rich in money and social recognition, but not at home – where it counts most. So, to answer your question, I saved you from the things that hurt you most – your wife and family. Those ingrates do not love or care about you. They're only concerned with themselves. It's not your fault. Here you will receive all of the affection and attention you've been missing. We, as a collective whole, will provide the safety, stability, and comfort of the family you've been lacking and crave."

"Exactly what qualifies *you* to make that decision?" My eyes widened as my head tilted to the right. Rational thought knew this man was not well in the head, but I wasn't sure how sick he was. Irrational thought wanted to beat his ass to a pulp for taking liberties he had no right to.

"Oh, I didn't make any decisions. God did. He told me what He wanted me to do for Him."

Woah. And, there's your answer. This psycho is a dangerous, unbalanced, religious nut bag. Proceeding with an abundance of caution is the only answer, because who knows exactly what he's capable of. Countless case studies have been written about lunatics just like Warren. All right. Use every ounce of knowledge inside of your brain to assess what's happening.

One – This is more than likely a cult group – the basement setup, the closet filled with uniform clothing, and the bolted windows. He's obviously the leader, but how many others are there?

Two – Does he have a second in command? Usually they don't, but sometimes they do. If yes, what's his or her mental state and capacity?

Three – The only way you're going to get out of here is to play into the game, gain his trust first, and the others will quickly follow suit. When he turns his back, strike.

Four – Jill was expecting you to be home when she

got off of work last night. Based on the sun exposure coming through the windows, it has to be late morning. She'll realize something is wrong, and will come looking for you. At minimum, she'll call the cops. Jill will do something, but until then you've got to remain level headed and patiently wait this out.

"God speaks directly to you?" I asked, taking a seat on the bed across from him.

"Yes."

"How long have you two been conversing?"

"About twenty or so years. We began communicating when I was in my early thirties."

"And *He* tells you to save people?" I leaned forward in an attempt to show this psychopath I was hanging on his every word, marveling over his direct line to God.

"Yes." He put his hand up to stop me from speaking. "You're going to ask how. It's simple. God sends me signs through various means. Sometimes it's visually – in person. Other times, like in your case, it's through the media. While in town picking up supplies, a magazine article about you caught my attention. That night I went home and God came to me. He instructed I find and bring you here." Warren removed a folded slice of paper from his back pocket. Handing it to me, he resumed speaking. "I went to the library – there's no internet here, and I researched you. The results revealed a situation far worse than I could have ever imagined. I knew beyond a shadow of a doubt you needed to be saved. Your family of origin – awful, but your wife is the foulest. Godless, soulless, sinners of the worst kind. Ugly, evil human beings, if one could even consider them that. They've used you, have taken advantage of your warm, loving nature, and have led you astray. God guided me to you so I could shepherd you to salvation. I will follow His orders."

The news snippet in question was a tabloid piece from several months ago. Obviously, this man had no idea what fake news consisted of. Not many choices were available. I could easily overtake him, but I wasn't sure of what would be waiting upstairs. How many people and what their mental capacities were remained an unknown. There was always the option to see who else resided here, then figure out how to make an escape. Lastly, waiting it out for Jillian to find me, also another tangible solution. But, perhaps the most logical course of action was a combination of all three extremes. The best way to tackle the here and now was to remain composed, assess the magnitude of all factors, and play along with Warren. In a few days I'd be out of here.

"I see. How do we go about doing that?" I inquired.

"Living here and *not* attempting to leave is the first step. Precautions are in place to prevent this from happening. It's strongly advised residents do not exit the property or else they'll deal with the ramifications, which I assure are not fun. For now, go get cleaned up, dressed, and come upstairs – the door will be unlocked. It's about lunchtime. You've got to be famished. Breaking bread is an excellent way to become acquainted with your new brothers and sisters. There's a selection of clothing in all sizes in the closet. Finding something to wear shouldn't be an issue." Warren stood.

"Great. Thanks," I replied, still sitting. Emotions are tricky little sneaks. You can smile to mask sadness, but appearances seep through expressions and body language sells you out every single time.

"You'll learn to be happy in your new home, but

only when you shed those awful people, those malefactors from your soul," Warren assured, before exiting.

In all of my life I'd never felt as defeated as I did in that moment. No plan. No means to an end. Nothing. This psychopath intended on keeping me here forever. Who knew what "precautions" he had in play to prevent anyone from leaving? Invisible electric fence? Armed whacko guards? Poison?

A deep exhale later, I knew the only way to get out of this alive and untouched would be to endure each second – watching, waiting, biding my time until the right moment to attack presented. View the problem in its entirety and devise a scheme from there. Everything happens for a reason. Everything. I was a firm believer in that spiritual sentiment. This time, this experience was no different. Riding the wave, weathering the rough surf, seeing where it took me was the only viable setup, for the moment. Hopefully this rough surf wasn't in horrible stormy seas.

Chapter 6

Jillian

I must've dozed off because I woke with a jolt due to the blaring sound of my cell phone ringing. The device vibrated in my hand screaming to be answered. Positioning myself upright, I pressed the talk button. Lose strands of my hair were carelessly tucked behind my ears.

"Nick?" I said.

"It's Liam. Everything okay over there?" Liam's deep voice inquired.

"I don't know," I replied, rubbing sleep from my eyes. "Hold on a second. I just woke up and have to check on something." Placing the phone on the cocktail table, I stood.

"Nick?" I called, walking through the kitchen, circling back to the informal living room, and then to his office, poking my head into the mudroom and opening the bathroom doors. "Nick? Are you home?"

Thinking perhaps he might be upstairs, I scaled the steps two by two. Sprinting down the hallways, I saw he wasn't there. Running back to the main floor, I peeked outside through the window beside the front door. His car was still gone. The master and guest room beds were made. Nick hadn't returned. Pressing the discarded cell phone to my ear, I panicked.

"You still there, Liam?"

"Yeah. What's going on, Jill?" I could hear the concern in his tone.

"Nick never came home last night. He was here when I left for the station and he told me he'd be here when I got off work. He said he was planning something for us. I assumed it was dinner or a romantic gesture of sorts, not him disappearing," I said quickly, trying to replay the highlights from our last conversation in my head. Never once did Nick suggest, nor allude to a vanishing act.

"Have you called him?"

"Of course. I've called, texted, and emailed. I've done everything short of send smoke signals. Nick's cell has to be off because calls go straight to voicemail. Texts and emails, no answer. I tracked his phone as well. The last place it pinged was at St. Luke's. I drove there and his Lexus was in the lot, but he wasn't around. The church was closed. Not a soul or vehicle were around *except* for his SUV. I parked and waited until a cop harassed me, giving me a field sobriety test, then telling me I couldn't stay there because it's trespassing. He didn't give a rat's ass about Nick. The moron advised that Nick was an adult who wasn't sick or crazy, and people go missing all the time. If he's not back in forty-eight hours I can go to my local precinct and file a missing person's report. This is going to sound nuts, but Liam, something's wrong. I just know it. It's a gut feeling. This isn't like Nick, especially now with him trying to make our marriage work. For shit's sake, we were in bed together all-day yesterday knocking boots. Why would he up and leave?"

"You don't have to wait forty-eight hours to file a

report with the police, Jill. We can go down to the station today and get the ball rolling."

"That's not what the cop said."

"He lied. It's a bullshit line they use in situations like this to get people to leave them alone. Trust me on this. If you don't believe me, call my brother. Randy will tell you the truth. He should know it after being on the job for almost forty years. Nick and you are celebrities, and the first forty-eight hours are the most crucial. Someone will listen and take a report. They might not be thrilled over having to do work, but they'll muddle through it."

"Do you think something happened to him? Be honest with me."

With a heavy sigh, he spoke. "I can't say for sure, Jill. It's not Nick's personality to disappear. Plus, wasn't he the one who wanted to put the divorce on hold? Usually when a couple is attempting to fix a broken marriage they don't walk away without telling the other. Is it odd he vanished? Yeah, especially after the tabloid story, but I'm sure there's an explanation. Let's not panic. I'll come pick you up and we can go to the police together. Give me twenty minutes. Okay?"

"I'll see you in a bit. Thanks, Liam."

"Of course. What are work fathers for?"

****

Thirty minutes later I found myself sitting on a beat up old wooden bench sandwiched between Liam and a sweaty, strung-out junkie who was handcuffed to the armrest. I'd been in police stations before for work related interviews, but never as someone who actually required help. Liam spoke to the desk sergeant, who uncaringly told us to take a seat and wait, mumbling someone would be with us shortly. Evidently, shortly to the police meant two hours, because that's how long I remained in Hell's Threshold.

"Winters?" A young, bald, somewhat fit cop asked, holding a piece of paper.

"That's us," Liam replied, taking my arm. "Come on, Jill. Look alive."

"Follow me," the officer ordered.

He led us down a narrow hallway to a flight of metal stairs. Once in the basement, the hum of cheap florescent lights filled the dingy space. Scuffed puke green linoleum floors did little to enhance the pealing blue and orange painted walls. A heavy stench of marijuana hung in the air. My nose crinkled at the earthy stink.

"Sorry about that. We just busted a dealer. Confiscated almost a hundred pounds of pot among other things," the cop explained as he opened a door which led to a beige room. A round, faux, dark wood table with several nasty, old, brown torn up vinyl chairs around it was the only thing inside of the enclosure. Once he shut the door, he spoke again.

"Take a seat." Plopping into one, he examined the paper in his hand. "Okay, so your husband is missing," he said, looking up.

I couldn't sit, so I paced – something I'd been doing a lot of. "Yes. Since yesterday night."

Liam held up his right hand in a "hold your horses" fashion. "I'm Liam Stevens. This is Jillian Winters. She anchors a nationally syndicated nightly news show which I produce. Her husband, Doctor Nicholas Winters, is an international bestselling, self-help author, who also hosts the number one talk Podcast in the country. Mrs. Winters was told early this morning by another officer to wait a full forty-eight hours before reporting him missing. We both know that's not a law or rule. Anyone can file a missing person's report in less time than that. With their celebrity status, we are, by no means, asking for special treatment, but what we are requesting is you get the ball rolling here. He's more at risk than most, mainly because, due to the nature of his work, he's surrounded by fans who potentially suffer from mental health illnesses. Nick is a psychotherapist, who I'm sure has treated many emotionally unstable individuals." Liam sat back in one of the rickety chairs, folding his arms against his chest.

"First things first, I'm Officer Wilson. Second, I'll gladly take a report and alert all personnel that your husband is missing. They'll be on the lookout and will call it in if they locate him. Walk me through the events that led up to his disappearance."

"We spent the day together, at our house. Before I left for work, he said he was planning something special for when I returned. I went to the studio, recorded my show, had a brief meeting with the station owner, then left. When I got home, he wasn't there. Pots were on the stove, pantry items were on the counter, and the dining room table was set. I tried calling him, but my calls went straight to voicemail. Texts and emails have gone unanswered as well. I tracked his last location from the GPS on his cell. It showed he was in the parking lot of St. Luke's Church. I went there. It was late. I found his Lexus – it appeared fine, at least visually it did. He wasn't around, so I waited. Then, a cop came and made me take a field sobriety test even after I explained the situation and that I hadn't had a drink or taken any mind-altering drugs. He told me to wait the mandatory forty-eight hours before filing a missing person report, suggesting sometimes people just leave, and demanded I vacate the premise because I was trespassing. He also threatened to have Nick's Lexus towed if it wasn't gone by morning. I went home, dozed off on the couch, Liam called, and now I'm here," I said in one long breath.

Wilson feverishly took careful notes. He must've been the new kid on the block, because most officers weren't as diligent.

"Did you and Mr. Winters have an argument prior to you leaving for work? Have you received any suspicious calls, texts, or emails before or after he disappeared? Any ransom requests? Signs of a struggle inside of the house? Is there anything you can think of, even if you deem it insignificant, that comes across as odd in the days leading up to today?"

I paused taking a second to glance at Liam. Did I tell him about the divorce? About my and Nick's dirty little secrets?

"It's okay, Jill," Liam encouraged. After years of working side by side the man could read my mind – an indescribable comfort.

"Nick and I were in the process of legally separating. We decided a few days ago to put a pin in that and try one more time. A member of the paparazzi took a few pictures of us entering my lawyer's office, then sold them to a tabloid. It's been all over the trash magazines. Since that day we've been fine – working on fixing our marriage."

Wilson looked up thoughtfully. "Can anyone confirm your whereabouts the night Mr. Winters disappeared?"

"Do you think *I* did something to him?" I asked shocked. My body stopped all forward motion and pivoted sharply in order to stare the dumb shit cop down. How dare he accuse me, of all people?

"I can vouch for her, as well as the station owner, her personal assistant, various on-air staff, and about three million viewers who watched the live show last night," Liam said.

"What about after the show ended? You went home?"

"I have around the clock security guards stationed at the house that told me Nick left the premises shortly after I did. In addition, I have a driver who drove me to and from work. The perimeter of the house is also wired with cameras. You're more than welcome to view the tapes."

"Does Mr. Winters have any enemies?"

"No," I snapped. Obviously this man had no clue who Nick was or what kind of person either.

"What Mrs. Winters is trying to say is, Doctor Winters is a beloved community member. If there's anyone who dislikes him or is holding a grudge against him, she's unaware," Liam said. His head lowered as he began to jot something down in a pocket-sized notebook. Once finished, he tore the page out. "This is a short list of people and their direct numbers at the station who saw Mrs. Winters the night Doctor Winters went missing. They will all be able to corroborate her story. If more names are required, let me know. I'd be happy to provide them."

"Thank you, Mr. Stevens. You've been very helpful. I'll type this up. Once that's done, it'll be circulated not only within our station, but to others in and around the state as well. If we hear anything, we'll let you know," Wilson said, standing, signaling the meeting was over.

"That's it? That's all you're going to do? My

husband is missing. He's not the type of person to just up and leave on a whim. Something is wrong. He's in danger, or hurt, or God only knows what. You're *not* listening. You're not understanding the severity of this situation," I demanded. My body moved swiftly to block the door so deputy dumbass couldn't leave until he saw things *my* way.

"Ma'am, if you'd like I can personally contact local hospitals and other precincts to see if he's there, but there's not much more we can do at this point. His name was run through our system and nothing pops up. His physical description along with his driver's license photo will be compared to all John Does. However, sadly people, even ones we believe wouldn't, sometimes leave. Maybe he decided he wanted to take the pin out of the separation and this is how he's doing it. We'll do what we can, but that's about all we can do. Sit tight. I'll make a few calls," Wilson answered before exiting the room.

"You've got to be kidding me, Liam," I seethed.

"Calm down, Jill. This is just the first step."

As much as my patience and nerves hated to admit it, he was right. That moment would commence the first of many necessary steps to bring Nick home.

Chapter 7

Nick

Being the only measurements of time inside of the house were clocks, I lost track of days and dates. Any marker of how long Warren held me against my will didn't exist inside his prison. In all fairness, Warren never struck or abused any of the abducted individuals, who were all legal aged adults. The youngest appeared to be in her late twenties. The oldest, a man, was in his early seventies. He treated them kindly, with a judgement free equality most humans lacked. Everything anyone could ever need had been provided. Three meals a day were prepared by whoever wished to cook. When no one wanted to, Warren would, but that didn't happen often. The abductees seemed to want to be where they were, happily engaging in daily busywork. About an hour before sunrise, the men would wake to shower and dress. When the men were done, the women began their morning rituals. As a whole, we'd go upstairs for a family style breakfast, attend Warren's Bible study group, do a few chores – mainly housework, eat lunch, perform outside tasks – gardening, mowing, weeding, cleaned up, ate dinner, then we'd have an hour of free time to socialize with the others. We were allowed to read books Warren selected, could draw or paint, knit, play board games, put together puzzles, and things of the like. Television or watching movies was not an option.

Often, I'd spend this period observing those around me. I'd inspect their behaviors, watch their body language, and listen in on their conversations. I was trying to get a sense of how brainwashed they'd become. Sometimes someone would approach me and start a conversation or extend an invitation to partake in an activity, most times I would, but other nights silently observing was my hobby of choice. After that we'd head down to the basement, wash up for bed, pray, then lights out. Every day resembled the day before. The only change was the weather. When it rained, they replaced outside work with an indoor project. Every few days Warren pulled each of us aside for a "talk." He'd open what he believed to be rich spiritual dialogues – a poor attempt at therapy to heal his "flock." I played along in an effort to figure him out. What I ascertained was these people were suffering from a severe case of Stockholm syndrome. Though Warren hadn't beaten or treated them poorly, he had one hell of a psychological hold over every single one of them.

If pressed, I'd surmise these people were damaged souls due to a multitude of sins from their former abusers. Warren "saved" them, brought them to a safe haven, then brainwashed them into his way of thinking. In my humble opinion, aside from Warren, all but one was treatable – Noah Lessor, Warren's cousin. That young man was off in more ways than countable. Noah rarely spoke, and when he did, it was always in rapid hushed tones, and only to Warren. The man, a hard worker, would simply stare at whoever was nearby. He wasn't what I'd consider a threat – standing at roughly five feet, seven inches, about one hundred and forty pounds, with sandy brown cropped hair, Noah appeared to be in his late thirties, and was rather nervous all of the time. It was almost as if he knew what was going on here was wrong and because of that, he lived in a constant state of fear he'd get caught. Additionally, he had some type of medical training. I observed him giving meticulous sutures to a middle-aged abductee after she sliced her hand while cutting a bagel.

Noah also conducted regular blood pressure tests on anyone over fifty-five. The oddest, creepiest part of Noah wasn't his lack of interaction with the others or his jittery nature, but rather his soulless eyes. When he'd glare in your direction it felt as if those two hazel orbs could bore a hole straight through you. He was probably the victim of horrific abuse as a child and adolescent, *and* Warren's first capture. In fact, he may have been the reason Warren started trying to rescue those around him. Perhaps guilt played a part – maybe he'd watched the ill treatment and did nothing about it, or he, himself, was victimized in the same fashion and didn't feel powerful enough to have his voice heard. Who knew? Both were onions with many, many layers to peel away before getting to the potent core.

Initially, I fought being there. I'd resist going upstairs to join the others, constantly planning an escape. Surely by now Jillian had alerted the authorities, but truthfully, what were they going to do? They'd write it off to marital abandonment due to the tabloid articles about our divorce. Quite possibly my name was entered into the system for cops to keep a lookout for, but in reality, they wouldn't, and where would they see me anyway? I wasn't allowed to leave the property.

Warren would come down daily and visit, enforcing

that this was the best place for me to be, and encouraging I try out this new life while embracing my surroundings. Several of the "flock" attempted chatting, but it wasn't until a woman, who I figured to be in her late twenties, began speaking with me nightly in private. Sarah would wait for me to exit the bathroom. When no one was looking, she'd pull me aside and purge her inner secrets in a childlike fashion. As she told the tale, her long fingers would twirl around strands of her hair. She'd giggle and whisper, always making sure to look up at me through her heavy eyelashes. I wasn't sure if she was seeking a new friendship or looking to embark upon a romantic relationship. On my first evening in the house, Warren warned against discussing our pasts – whatever happened back then didn't matter or exist anymore, and brothers and sisters were forbidden to exchange physical intimacies. Never-the-less, Sarah was human and humans had needs and desires. On my side of the equation, no attraction existed. Only sorrow over her story.

Warren had taken her years ago. She'd been "rescued" from her physically and emotionally abusive husband, Seth. She had no children and had worked as a public-school teacher in Manhattan. Sarah said Warren "saved" her as she took a shortcut down a back alley one rainy evening during the late fall. When I questioned her as to why she was breaking the house rules by telling me this personal information, she explained she knew who I was and felt comfortable in my presence. After listening to Sarah's nightly ramblings, I felt if I had to be stuck here for who knew how long, the time spent in Purgatory should be used in a more productive fashion. Sulking and plotting would have to wait. So, using my knowledge and talents, I set out to help these lost, poor, broken people. They didn't need to be controlled by Warren to heal. Sadly, they didn't know any better.

"Brother Nick?" Sarah said one morning when we were alone in the kitchen preparing breakfast.

The rest were still downstairs preparing for the day, and Warren and Noah had left for town to pick up supplies. Warren and Noah slept upstairs in their own rooms. Both had access to a television and a computer. Despite Warren saying the house was internet and media free, while tidying the upstairs a few days ago, both doors had been unlocked. Curiosity took over, and a careful venture inside of each's personal space occurred. It didn't shock or surprise me. You'd think they'd keep the devices hidden, but no. There they were, bold as brass in the middle of the room. Granted, the second floor was off limits and no one dare defy Warren and sneak up there, but I'd been given instructions that afternoon before they left to give the second floor a good once over. The only logical explanation was Warren had to keep tabs on the biological family members and friends of his "flock" to make sure they weren't buzzing around, potentially creating a problem. In their rush to vacate the house, they probably forgot to lock up. I didn't dare attempt to touch anything out of being unsure over when they'd return, if anyone was nearby, or what the consequences might be if caught.

"Yes," I said, and turned. I placed the frying pan in my hand on the counter providing her with my total attention.

She looked down, then up innocently through those long eyelashes. Initially, I wasn't sure of her motives, but after close consideration the doe eyed expression seemed to be her coy way of showing attraction. In fact, as the days drew on it wasn't a big secret she wanted me as a partner, not another house brother. The others saw it too. A few had even commented on it privately. Warren had not – yet. I immediately shut it down, because giving this girl the wrong impression wasn't something of interest, nor okay to do. For her this setup was a life sentence – something she welcomed. For me, hell no. Returning to Jillian as soon as possible was my goal – my *only* goal. This was *not*, and would *never* be, my forever. However, making her feel as if I cared, which I did, just not in the fashion she desired, and creating a healthy environment was key in the recovery process.

"Do you think I'm pretty?" Her big, brown eyes instantly dropped as she examined her shoes. She wanted to be in an atmosphere where she believed a good, safe person held interest in her on a higher level than "flock" member. Not having been able to accurately assess her psychologically, my thoughts kept returning to this woman's lack of self-confidence and inferiority issues.

Crap. Tread lightly with this one.

"I think you're smart, talented, gifted, giving, caring, and kind – qualities that supersede external beauty any day of the week. That fades. Who you are inside lasts a lifetime. You're also a fantastic cook, skilled knitter, and amazing gardener. The blankets you made for the house are awesome, and you were the only one able to bring the rose bush in the yard back to life," I answered with a smile.

She didn't say anything. Her fallen expression spoke such loud volumes any series of words wouldn't have done justice for the dialogue going on inside of her head at that very moment.

"Sarah," I said, placing a hand on her shoulder. "I have a wife. We took vows. As long as we're married I will not go against those promises."

"Brother Warren saved you from *her* and her *evil* ways. She shouldn't be a part of your life anymore. You have to let her go," she yelled. "And it's Sister Sarah, *not* Sarah," she added, before storming out of the room.

This is bad. Very bad. Damn it.

Pissing off an unhinged, mentally imbalanced cult member was never a good way to start any day – ever, and an even worse way to gain her or anyone in the house's trust.

Chapter 8

Jillian

Two weeks – fourteen long days passed since Nick disappeared. Nothing had been done to locate him. His Lexus was towed to a local police impound yard. I'd been told a team had combed the SUV and nothing out of the ordinary presented. After that, calls and emails to the station were ignored. Not knowing what to do, but realizing too much time had passed, I reached out to my personal attorney, Charles Downey. His first reaction was for me to hire a private investigator, which I contemplated, but then he suggested holding a press conference. This would not only encourage the general public to be on the lookout, but would force the police's hand to get off their asses and do something, utilizing their technology – technology tax payers such as myself, funded. This move might also inspire the FBI to get involved. With more resources on my side, finding Nick would become easier. I hoped.

"Before you pull the trigger on this and give me the go ahead, I must warn you, for as many pros this tactic may provide, there will be the same, or more, amount of cons. All of your and Nick's hidden secrets and dirty laundry run the risk of being exposed. Are you sure this is what you want to do?" Charles asked.

"Yes. Nick must be found. He needs to come home,"

I answered, not caring which skeletons flew out of the closet. The discomfort would be well worth it. Nick's safe return far outweighed the world knowing we both committed adultery, or put a pin in a potential divorce.

"All right. I'll set everything up and will alert the police," he said, and hung up.

Twenty-four hours later, I stood on the front steps of my home addressing the nation. Camera lights flashed; video equipment rolled. It seemed as if every media outlet showed up. To my right stood Liam and Charles. To my left, the Commissioner of the Nassau County Police Department, and a team leader assigned to this case from the FBI. The second Charles informed the precinct of the presser, within the hour he received a call from the FBI. Charles informed them that after the conference we'd sit down to discuss matters with Special Agent Timothy Wilder. For the moment, Wilder and his office had been briefed and had settled into a nearby hotel.

"For those of you who do not know me, I'm Jillian Winters. I stand here today asking the public for help. My husband, Doctor Nicholas Winters, has been missing for fifteen days. The last time I saw him he was here, at our home. I was leaving for work. It was around six o'clock in the evening. Nick's black Lexus SUV was found at St. Luke's Roman Catholic Church in town abandoned. It's to my understanding none of his personal effects, such as his cell phone, which has been turned off since the night he went missing, were in the vehicle. Calls, emails, and text messages have gone unanswered. The last traceable ping came from the church parking lot. His SUV was intact, with no signs of foul play. The police, and now FBI, have been actively investigating, but still can't locate Nick. I fear he's in danger, and I humbly ask you, the public, for assistance with finding him. If you've seen him, think you have, or know of his whereabouts, please come forward, immediately. There is a reward which I have solely funded for any information leading to Nick's safe return." I paused. "Nick, if you're watching, please know I am doing *everything* in my power to bring you home. If it's the last thing I do, you *will* return to me, alive and well. To any and all persons who may have my husband, please, do the right thing. Turn yourself in. Yes, there will be a price to pay for your actions, but the longer you wait, the worse the consequences will be.

"I love Nick. I miss my husband. We may not have a perfect fairytale life, but he's my world, and…" I said, no longer able to choke back tears. Liam placed his strong hand on my shoulder and squeezed. Turning, I buried my face in his chest. I couldn't take, nor properly handle the unexpected severe rise of emotions. Usually, I was in control, saving the weeping for later when I was alone. Sobbing uncontrollably into Liam's periwinkle blue, cotton, dress shirt, I couldn't stop. My makeup ran down my cheeks, staining the fabric. Regaining composure seemed impossible. My arms shook and my legs went weak. If it wasn't for Liam's firm grip, I would've hit the floor, knees first. The sound of his steady heartbeat and the hum of the soft wind drowned out the bright lights, snapping cameras, and reporters screaming questions in my general direction.

"Good morning. I'm Nassau County Police Commissioner, Dan Lindsay, and the gentleman to my left is FBI Special Agent Tim Wilder. An active joint investigation between the Nassau County PD, Suffolk

County PD, NYPD, various other surrounding municipalities, and the FBI is underway as we seek answers in the disappearance of Doctor Nicholas 'Nick' Winters," Lindsay began, but I wasn't listening. His recount to the public of what was already known provided no closure or resolution. He spoke for roughly five minutes before turning the microphone over to Wilder. I simply stood beside Liam, clinging to his arm, and sobbing.

"I won't waste anyone's valuable time by repeating what Commissioner Lindsay already stated. The only thing I'd like to add is, this case is being treated as an abduction, meaning we have reason to believe Doctor Winters was taken against his will. The area around St. Luke's Church has been thoroughly combed. Security cameras are being checked, and Doctor Winters' black Lexus SUV is currently undergoing further analysis in addition to what Nassau County PD has conducted. Several leads are being followed, but as of right now we have no suspects.

"Like Mrs. Winters said earlier, we ask you, the public, to come forward with any information you may have. Even if you believe it to be small, it may end up being the key to solving this case. There is a one-million-dollar reward for any information leading to Doctor Winters's safe return, provided by Mrs. Winters. You can call the hotline number, or send a tip via email. Phone numbers and web addresses are listed on the flyers you've all been given. These flyers will also be circulated throughout the Tri-State Area, posted on social media sites, as well as uploaded and sent to police departments around the country. With a fifteen day lag time, Doctor Winters could be anywhere. All communication will remain anonymous. We have time for a few questions," Wilder said.

"Why is this information coming out now, after fifteen days?" A male reporter shouted.

"Initial assessments from the Nassau Country PD suggested Doctor Winters left on his own free will. In light of recent developments, we have reason to believe that was not the case, which is why the FBI has been called in and the status of this case has been upped to active abduction," Wilder answered. "You, the woman in the red top."

"Can you elaborate on what made the FBI upgrade the status of the case?"

"No, not at this time. The gentleman in the brown tweed coat all the way in the back."

"Have any arrests been made?"

"No. Last question. You, lady with the yellow and blue boots."

"What's Mrs. Winters' involvement in this? Is she being questioned because of the divorce?"

"Mrs. Winters is not a suspect. Her alibi for the evening in question has been checked out and confirmed. As for Doctor and Mrs. Winters' personal life, that's none of your business. No more questions." With that, Wilder turned on his heel and walked back into my house.

"Thank you for your time and for joining us today. That's all for now. We'll provide updates to the press when they are available," Commissioner Lindsay spoke, following Wilder's lead.

"Come on, Jill. Let the police worry about getting these vultures off of your property," Liam said, placing his hand on the small of my back, and escorting me into the foyer.

"Mrs. Winters, I'd like to speak if you have a moment. Mr. Stevens and Mr. Downey are more than welcome to join," Wilder requested.

With a nod I walked into Nick's office and closed the door. Wilder, Liam, and Charles all sat beside one another on rich, port wine colored, leather wingchairs. I took a seat behind Nick's massive mahogany desk waiting for Wilder to speak. Leaning back in the oversized office chair proved empowering. Until that moment, Nick's picky nature over the setup of his space never made sense. When he sat here he felt in control. A secret smile formed over how fantastic of a hold he had over human nature, more specifically, his own.

"I know this must be a difficult time, but I'd appreciate it if you could walk me through the events forty-eight hours prior to Doctor Winters disappearance. It may be hard, but try to recall every detail possible, even if you don't think it matters," he said, taking out a cheap, flimsy notebook, and opening it to a blank page. His slender left hand was poised with pen.

To the best of my recollection I told him everything that happened from the time we met at the lawyer's office to the rude cop in the church parking lot.

"So you and Doctor Winters were separated?"

"No. Yes, but not really. We both had lawyers and were actively discussing a divorce, but at that last meeting he was the one who asked to speak with me in private. Nick wanted to work on our issues, putting the separation on hold. I agreed, because I felt the same way. Our attorneys told us that was totally fine and wished us the best. Both offices placed a stay on the case. But, all the while we were going back and forth through our lawyers we remained in the same house. We existed in different areas and slept in different bedrooms."

"Mr. Downey, are you representing Mrs. Winters in the divorce matter?" Wilder asked.

"I was."

"You're aware of the state of the Winters' marriage prior to Doctor Winters' disappearance?"

"Yes."

"Care to comment on it? Can you shed light on anything?"

"I can, but due to attorney/client privilege I won't. Not without a court order. However, I will comment, *for the record*, violence, threats, or anything which would require a restraining order was never an issue. Additionally, I can confirm that everything Mrs. Winters has said today is the truth."

"I understand, but with this being treated as an abduction, whatever you can offer beyond that would be most helpful and useful in bringing Doctor Winters home faster." He paused thoughtfully. "I suppose what I'm asking is, can anyone in this room offer the names of any possible persons of interest? Are there any proverbial skeletons we should be made aware of before the press finds out and makes it into something it's not, potentially complicating or interfering with our investigation?"

Charles and Liam both glanced at me. The ball was in my court if I wanted to own the affairs or not.

"For the past several years I've engaged in a handful of extra-marital affairs. Nick had one as well. I'd be happy to provide all of their names and contact information, but I highly doubt any of them have anything to do with this. I don't know about Nick's indiscretion, but all of the men I socialized with were married celebrities who wouldn't want it to get out," I answered boldly. Eventually it would come out in the wash now that the press and public were involved. The press would dig and stalk, while the public would start social media amateur sleuth groups blindly blaming anyone their simpleton minds could fathom.

"Okay. Can I have those names, please?"

"Jake Forsyth, the actor. Ryder McCullum, the author. Marc Davies, the news anchor. Todd Cooper, the sports commentator. Mitchel Chambers, the stuntman. Kelly Greenly was Nick's personal assistant, and the only person I'm aware of that he cheated with," I said, scribbling down the names and last known telephone numbers.

"Are you currently having an affair with anyone at the moment?"

"No."

"When was the last time you did?"

"I don't know. Six, eight months ago? It was with Jake Forsyth."

"Have you had any communication with any of these men? Has Doctor Winters been in contact with Ms. Greenly?"

"No, I haven't. We're all public figures with spouses. Some have children. It was a low key, private thing. When one of us is in town, we may or may not reach out. If it's a yes, then we'll meet up at a hotel. If it's a no, it's a no. Period. As for Nick, it's to my understanding he's not, but I can't say for sure when was the last time he spoke to or saw Kelly." My stomach churned at the thought of Kelly and Nick still speaking.

"I'll have to question everyone involved, but don't worry. It will be done with the highest amount of privacy and the utmost respect, free of judgement. No one will even know."

"That's fine, but I must warn you. If this does get out, I, and whoever is accused, will deny the hell out of all of the allegations; as will our public relations teams. We have reputations to protect and families to maintain," I cautioned.

"Understood. The FBI isn't interested in breaking up families or ruining lives over affairs. Have you received any phone calls, texts, or emails demanding money? Any blackmail? Anything at all feel or appear off? Has your security crew noticed anything out of the ordinary?"

"Nothing, but feel free to speak with security on your way out. Raul, my head of security, is currently on the clock. I'd touch base with him first as he was working the evening Nick didn't come home."

"Last question before I take off. Do you know who Paris Rosen or Shelly Rockland are?"

"I don't think so. Those names don't ring a bell. Why?"

"We found their information in Doctor Winters' call log. He'd recently been in communication with them."

"No clue." My curiosity piqued. Who were these women? Affairs? Lawyers? Professional contacts? Friends?

"If you can think of anything else, please reach out. My team and I are staying at the North Shore Oaks Hotel," Wilder said, standing, and handing me a business card.

"Is Mrs. Winters a suspect?" Charles asked, still sitting.

"Not at this moment. Her alibi checked out, but no

stone can be left unturned, so the Bureau is going to ask if we can search the house and take anything we may deem of interest to our lab for testing. You can say no, but I will return with a court order. Dealer's choice."

"Of course you can. If there's something in this house that could lead you to Nick, by all means tear the place apart," I said, without waiting for Charles's input. I had nothing to hide. Maybe Charles thought otherwise, but there wasn't a thing I could think of that would incriminate me. I'd already admitted the worst – the affairs.

"Thank you. I'll let the agents know it's a go. We'll be in touch with Mr. Downey before we return this way it's a convenient time for all of us, and we can handle this discreetly without press involvement." With that he exited, leaving Charles, Liam, and myself in silence.

"Are you sure that's a wise move?" Charles questioned, breaking the ice.

"Yeah," I replied, shrugging. "It makes the most amount of sense since *I didn't do it*. There's nothing to conceal. Plus, if we do it this way, we can control it – no press, no tabloid stories, no public speculation. They'll come in quietly and leave the same way."

"I agree with Jill, but they're going to snag everything and who the hell can say when it'll be returned? Give me your work laptop and cell phone. Give them your personal electronics. You're going to need something to communicate with the outside world in case Nick calls," Liam said.

"Good idea," I answered, turning my attention to Nick's filing cabinet. "Let's comb through this as well while you're here. Anything suspicious we shred or hide. Yes?"

Liam nodded.

"I didn't hear any of that." Charles turned away. "I'll let you know when the Feds want to search the house. In the meantime, if anything pops up, call. *Immediately*."

"Will do."

"Do *not* speak with anyone, Jill. No press. No personal chats with friends, and *especially* with anyone from Nick's family. Not even Beau. I'm aware of their perception of situations *and* of you. Surely, they've been filled in on Nick's disappearance. If not, they live under a damn rock. Whether they watched the presser or their staff has informed them, it doesn't matter. The Winters clan will be out in full force – pitchforks in hand, fully sharpened. The press, neighbors, friends, colleagues too. Anyone you've ever given a sideways glance to – be on alert. Mouth shut. Also, don't let what others say get under your skin. I highly advise you stay away from the television, social media sites, and newspapers. My team will be on the lookout if anything gets out of hand. If it does, we will handle it. *Not* you. Got it?" Charles warned.

"Yes."

An hour later, after Charles left and every drawer in Nick's office thoroughly searched, Liam collected my personal items and smuggled them out of the house. Alone, I found myself sitting in the family room, in silence. Phones had been shut off to avoid the temptation of answering them. Playing with the television remote, I gave up and pressed the on button. How bad could it be?

Chapter 9

Nick

A handful of days passed since Sarah's feeble attempt at seduction. The time had been spent walking on eggshells around everyone. Though Warren hadn't said anything, he knew. Sarah told him what happened and what I'd said about Jillian. Reading the tell-tale signs wasn't difficult. This smirk of sorts wore boldly across her face giving the secret away. I didn't stop conducting my mental research, but I did go about obtaining the information differently. A coyer style was utilized. Instead of striking up conversations with the others, I returned to silent observation from afar. No notes were taken because nothing in this house was private. Either a resident or Warren himself more than likely went through the bedside notebooks given to each member of his sick family. Besides, his attention was already on me due to the slip. Risking doing anything else, adding to his suspicions was too risky.

"Brother Nicholas. We must speak. In private," Warren said one evening during free hour.

He entered the den, closed the door, and sat. I'd been in there alone for about a half hour pretending to read some Dollar Store book about planting seasons.

"How can I help you?" I asked cautiously, shutting the book, and bracing for the shit storm ahead.

Crap. Here it comes.

"This may be difficult to hear, and please know everyone in this house – your brothers and sisters, are all here for you." He paused, looking down and to the left. "Yesterday, Jillian was in a car accident and was killed. It was all over the news and the papers. I happened to see a copy of a newspaper at the market in town."

"What? Let me see it," I demanded in disbelief. No. There was no way anything like that happened. Not to Jillian. No. He had to be lying. She was one of the best drivers alive; cautious to a fault, adhering to every rule in the Department of Motor Vehicle's Handbook. After what happened to her parents she always took being on the road seriously.

"You know I do not bring the outside world into this house, Brother Nicholas. Newspapers, magazines, the internet, television – none of that garbage has any place in this home. I can say this much. A drunk driver blew through a red light crashing into the car she was in. She was a passenger in the front seat. The intoxicated driver has since been arrested. The individual Jillian was with is in the hospital and should recover. It was quick and painless. She's free now, and I'm confident God will dole out a fitting punishment for the person responsible."

"No. I don't believe you. Prove it. Go back into town and get the paper," I said, standing, and pacing the space. Everything around me suddenly felt surreal. Like I was living in a dream.

"As you wish. I'll be back," Warren said.

Had I not returned to a seated position, my body would've collapsed. I couldn't speak, think, or perform any basic task. My limbs screamed to find strength, but none existed within me. If even the tiniest amount of power was summoned, the rest of my form possessed the potential to barrel through Warren and the others. Surely town wasn't too far away, and even if it was, I'd run to Jillian, wherever she was. I'd find her. Whatever it took; it didn't matter.

"I had Brother Noah visit the market to locate a copy. It's all here. I'm sorry," Warren spoke calmly, re-entering the room, handing me a piece of newspaper, and exiting.

There in black and white was a picture of Jillian, a shot of the wreckage, and an article explaining the horrific details. Best summed up – Jillian was in the front seat of a car driven by an unidentified young male heading west toward the city. The vehicle was slammed into by an intoxicated driver who ignored a red light in a heavily populated part of Queens. She died on impact. Thoughts like I never experienced raced through my head at such a rapid rate I didn't think I'd ever be able to keep up, never mind process anything. The most interesting musing? Warren did this. He killed my wife to make sure I'd stay in line, so I'd forget about her. I couldn't be one hundred percent certain he or that psychopath cousin of his was behind it, it was simply a gut feeling they were. Her passing was too convenient, timed too properly after the Sarah incident. An anger so dark, so black, so rooted in my soul bubbled, boiled, and was seconds away from spilling over. The pent-up rage required an immediate outlet. Without thinking, my arms wildly swept across the contents of the small corner desk. A primal, guttural scream erupted. My eyes only saw red as the floor lamp, hung painting, even the recliner, were flung around the space. Beads of sweat formed on my forehead, rolling down my face, and stinging my eyes.

My clothing stuck to my body. My shoulders heaved, and my fists clenched. My breath was heavy and hard. A heat so intense exploded from my core. Standing in the middle of the room, panting like a man who'd just run a three-minute mile, my body finally relaxed. My legs gave up, buckling. The threadbare Persian rug cushioned the fall. Knees to my chest, my head dropped. What was left to fight for? Nothing. Warren may have orchestrated this, but it was my actions which caused it.

Not true, a small, but strong voice whispered from within. Granted, I'd never been a vengeful person, but people change. This moment shifted the invisible line between right and wrong. Warren would pay for this. He'd pay dearly.

****

Several days passed with Warren and his "flock" keeping a sizable distance from me. Finally, he took the lead, opening the lines of communication. During that time my being craved solitude, but the strange thing was, I'd never felt so alone before. This sense of isolation consumed me, eating away at my insides until an epiphany struck. This was exactly what Warren wanted. He needed me to feel excluded so I'd require them, which caused me to wonder how many times he'd done this to the others. When one feels like a person with nothing left to lose, you're far easier to break, to shove back into line. The time spent in seclusion wasn't wasted, though. A plan of action slowly came into creation. In order for him to fully trust me again, I'd have to show him I'd come around. That I accepted Jillian's untimely fate. He'd have to see a shattered shell of a man before him. Once I was able to establish this scenario, getting into his and the other's minds wouldn't be too terribly difficult. With each passing day, opportunities to join in various household activities were taken advantage of, until eventually the tension broke.

"How are you doing, Brother Nicholas?" Warren asked when I was unaccompanied in the yard raking leaves. Based off the temperature, weather, shorter days, foliage colors, and nature of the work, autumn had arrived. Being dates and days didn't exist here, the month remained an unknown.

"All right. And, yourself?" I asked, stopping, and leaning on the handle of the rake.

"It's only natural to feel deep emotions after a tragic loss. We can discuss it if you'd like." He kept ample space showing caution, but his tone and body language revealed a calm being. Part of him feared my dark side that he'd witnessed in the den the night he dropped the bomb. Chances were, Warren never expected that kind of reaction, especially from a person like myself. Therapists were supposed to always remain level and when their axis shifted, they were supposed to be skilled and trained enough to keep themselves in check. Such a stupid, common misconception. We were humans with natural reactions to stimulus around us, just like everybody else walking this Earth.

"Thank you, but I'm okay. Really. The news was shocking, to say the least. Though no one deserves to leave this world before their time, and I refuse to speak ill of the dead, time stops for no man. God always has a reason. Who am *I* to challenge *Him*? Who am *I* to resist *His* will?" I shrugged, conversing as matter-of-factly as possible.

"Too true. Is there anything I, or we, can do to assist you in any way?" He moved closer, suggesting he felt confident I wouldn't go all gorilla again.

"I appreciate the offer, but no, thank you. I'm doing fine, Brother Warren. We must always be moving forward. I intend to do just that." My neck nodded more than a bobble head doll. Maintaining a megawatt smile was the worst part. Deep down I wanted to strangle this piece of crazy shit. My fingers craved the ability to wrap themselves tightly around his windpipe, watching their power force the life out of his lungs.

"You have no idea how happy I am to hear your faith has been restored. At times it will waver, but we must always believe in the greater good, the bigger picture."

Controlling my fists to not slam into his smug, ruddy face was quite a feat.

"Amen," I replied, propping the gardening tool against the side of the house or else it would've been used as a weapon. I took a seat on a nearby deck chair. Warren followed. "I will say this much. The experience, the psychological process – though unique for everyone, was commanding, but yet expressive and profound in such a fashion much was learned."

"Oh? How so?" Warren postured in. His elbows rested on his knees, as his chin propped on top of his folded hands.

"You learn a lot about yourself, life, and God in those controlling, broken, beautiful moments. Now, some may see the loss of faith as awful, sinful, but I disagree. That shaky frame of time shows you that He is truly there, always. His love can always be felt. His desire is for us to fall from grace so he can guide us back with a greater strength." I silently prayed he was buying this epic line of bullshit. Yes, I'd always been a firm believer in things happening for a reason, and perhaps there was a divine force secretly at work behind the scenes, but in the end, we make the decisions based off of knowledge of what option will provide the best outcome. If one sits waiting for a sign from above, there's a tremendous chance they'll be sitting, twiddling their thumbs for quite a while. However, at this current impasse, supporting Warren's narrative was my only choice for survival.

"Couldn't agree more." He affirmed.

"The entire happening made me think," I continued. My head turned away from his general direction and faced forward. This subtle move indicated the next string of crap coming from my mouth would come across as a musing, not a plan to take him down. Reclining in the chair, a deep inhale and even longer exhale occurred. My shoulders dropped as my body prepared to sell my lies to this sicko.

"May I inquire what about?" Warren's left eyebrow raised. His interest was piqued.

"Yes. Of course you may. My brothers and sisters – all of us here, have been on my mind. I'm aware of how we all became a family – God's will through your mind and heart, but if I hadn't experienced the passing of my wife, a true cause of remarkable grief, my recent epiphany wouldn't have arisen." I turned to face him directly. "Brother Warren, do you understand the weight that's been lifted from my shoulders? How much lighter I feel? How the world and all of God's miracles in it are visible, bolder, and brighter? It's as if fresh life has been pumped into my veins. I can breathe for the first time. So, I think to myself, what if I can do this for the others? The ones who haven't felt this, because I know not everyone we love inside of our home has experienced this beautiful gift from God, *yet*." Making sure my tone reflected my desired sentiment of excitement wasn't as difficult as I expected. The spot-on acting impressed the hell out of me. I almost believed myself for a flash.

"This is wonderful, Brother Nicholas. I'm thrilled beyond measure to hear you say this. I, too, have noticed some days our brothers and sisters tend to have 'moments' where the past creeps back into the forefront of their minds. They forget they're safe and loved now. Protected from the outside world which unfairly beat them down. How do you propose we help our family?" One didn't have to examine his face closely to see the wheels turning inside of his warped, psychotic brain.

"I'm so glad you asked." My grin beamed from ear to ear.

Hook. Line. Sinker.

"Grant me the right to help them. Allow me to use my gift and talent as a psychotherapist to guide them along the right path to see the light. I don't believe God makes mistakes. I've always said and felt that. *He* gave *you* a precious means of communicating with Him. This led you to me. My wife's passing was the final piece of the puzzle. My self-awareness has aided me to this point. The knowledge I've acquired over the years from school, life, and treating others in private practice has contributed to getting me to where I needed to be, which is right here."

"I don't know. To make them relive and dig up the past doesn't sound like a good idea. It could lead to bad things. Having a momentary flashback is one thing, but actively extracting memories? I'm going to have to say no." Warren pulled away. He was losing interest. It was time to turn up the charm, but in order to do that I had to play a low move. Something I didn't want to do.

"With all due respect, I disagree and will explain why. First, if Sister Sarah was whole within herself she wouldn't have inquired if I found her attractive or attempted to come on to me in the kitchen some weeks ago – which, might I add, is against house rules. When I declined the advances she became upset. Her reaction to the rejection wasn't what I'd consider balanced. Her need for validation is a byproduct of a lingering past." I broke off, carefully examining his expression and body language. He shifted in the chair. His stubby fingers scratched his head. "Also, Brother Noah doesn't join in often, if ever. He tends to hang back, watching the others. He's been asked by pretty much all of us at one time or another to participate in activities, but he always looks away, down, or hastily leaves the room. It is my professional opinion that he is still wrestling with inner demons himself. Perhaps he doesn't feel worthy of our love, time, or friendship. How sad is that? Aren't we all entitled to those simple life pleasures? Don't we all, as people with beating hearts and influential souls, crave and deserve to feel loved, wanted, and accepted? These are basic human rights. Please, Brother Warren, allow me to assist them. Let me share God's light the same way you have."

After a few minutes of quiet reflection, he spoke. "Okay, but on one condition. I get to be present for these one-on-one or group sessions."

"Unfortunately, I can't allow that, but what I can agree to is sharing everything with you privately, behind closed doors, weekly. If you're there our family who sees you as our leader, which you are, a father figure of sort, may not speak as freely due to not wanting to upset, hurt, or let you down. The key to what I'd like to do is getting that weight off everyone's backs. Allowing them to finally shed the pain of the past, in a safe, controlled environment," I countered.

"All right. Fridays, after dinner, while our brothers and sisters are cleaning up, we will take an hour or so to discuss what's going on in each session. You can use the room behind the den in the back of the house as a sanctuary. It's far enough away from the main living space that no one will be able to hear what's going on. Everyone will be instructed to refrain from using the den while you're doing your thing. You'll have complete privacy. I will speak with them tonight and you may begin your work tomorrow morning."

Reaching over and placing my hand over his, I made sure to make perfect, solid eye contact.

"You won't regret this. You'll see. This will be the best thing for all of us. I promise," I said, knowing no truer words had ever been spoken.

****

"So, Sarah, how have you been?" I asked, relaxing in the armchair I'd moved from the den into the small back room Warren had provided. Over the past several days, I transformed the space into a makeshift office with a nearly threadbare chocolate brown suede love seat, a small, rickety, wooden desk, and the old armchair. The request to brighten up the space had been happily met two days later with three gallons of paint, primer, and several pieces of framed artwork from the "flock." Working rapidly, five of the men and I finished the job in record time. Besides attempting to give off the illusion the space was harmless, a judgement free zone, I'd have total access to make sure Warren or Noah hadn't planted any recording devices. Each time I entered the room, I'd sweep it from top to bottom, making sure nothing had been slipped in, on, or under something. Warren could not, under any circumstances, be privy to what happened behind closed doors.

"It's *Sister* Sarah," she snapped. Her arms tightly folded across her chest while her legs locked at the ankle. Obviously, she was still pissed off over what happened, or rather what hadn't happened between us. In order for this to work, this session required a lot of soft touch finessing.

"All right. How have you been, *Sister Sarah*?" I rephrased.

"Fine. Can I go now? I don't want to do this, mainly because it's a stupid waste of time. There's absolutely nothing wrong with me."

"You're free to leave whenever you'd like. I'm not forcing anyone to stay, *especially* if being in this room is causing any sort of negative emotion, which clearly, for you, it is." I leaned forward and looked down on the desk. My right index finger traced the rim of a coffee mug before I made eye contact – something Sarah desperately desired. "We can't move on if you're still living in the past."

"You don't know anything about me." Sarah's eyelids narrowed. For a brief moment her cold, hard stare reminded me of Jillian. A pang of pain entered my heart, causing a slight wince in response. There wasn't a day that Jillian wasn't in at least three quarters of my thoughts. The good times, hell, even the bad ones played on a loop. Each memory was more than welcomed, but each memory caused the grieving process to begin again. My beautiful wife – gone. Ripped from my arms without warning, without a simple goodbye.

"I think I do. Deepest apologies if I'm out of line, *but* from what I've gathered, you're angry and not just at me, but with something or someone else. Your ego – your sense of self-esteem and self-importance, is hurt. We can work to heal that, or feel free to go on your merry way. The call is yours, Sister Sarah."

"I'm not an idiot. I know what an ego is. Before coming here, I was an elementary school teacher. I have a Master's Degree in education." Sarah's tone and expression hadn't budged, but she'd cracked a door open. Not much, but enough for me to get inside of her head.

"Education is a noble field. It's also a difficult one. A teacher is given at least twenty children from all walks of life, who learn differently, have diverse needs and personalities, and so on. It's up to the educator to reach all of them at once." I rested back in the chair, taking a brief moment to study her. A slight sense of relaxation seeped into her eyes.

Keep talking, Nick. You've got this in the bag.

"I remember this one time, many years ago, a colleague asked if I'd be interested in teaching a college class on abnormal psychology. I don't know what I was thinking when I agreed to do it. Guess I thought it'd be easy. How hard could teaching a bunch of adults be? Wow, was I in over my head. All of the lesson planning, grading, paper reading, while trying to impact each and every student in the class was exhausting, but rewarding." I finished my speech with an easy, careless chuckle and smile.

"Did you teach the next semester?" Sarah was captivated. The suggestion of an intimate conversation enchanted her.

"Good grief, no." I laughed loudly. The emotional response was overdone, but since she wanted to feel engaged, she'd believe it, which she did. Hook. Line. Sinker. I had her the moment she giggled.

"It can be difficult some days, but I always loved it. Over the course of one hundred eighty-three days, my students would become my children. Come June, it was always so difficult to say goodbye and let them go to the next grade, but for the year, I made sure they were safe, secure, happy, and loved coming to school." Sarah smiled brightly at the thought of her former life.

"Ever miss that?" I mused.

"Sure, every now and again, but being here is the better option." She repositioned her hips. To the trained eye, one could clearly see her inner pain breaching the surface.

"Want to talk about it? I've been told I'm an excellent listener," I said softly, reaching out and covering her hand with mine.

"I shouldn't," Sarah whispered, fighting a wave of tears.

"It's okay to cry, Sister Sarah. It's a natural expression. It's full of healing benefits. When Brother Warren told me about my wife, I cried, I got angry, and I allowed that to happen so I could come out on the other side, whole. The simple act of shedding tears helped bring clarity. I was able to view my previous life plainly for what it was, then I grieved that. Now, the man you see sitting here before you today is balanced and healthy," I encouraged. Inserting myself, humanizing the situation to show we were different, yet the same could only help.

"It's a long story. I doubt you really care or want to hear it." She glanced down and away, avoiding all eye contact, but she didn't move away from my touch.

"That's where you're wrong. I *do* care and *do* want to hear what you have to say, but if you're not ready, or don't feel comfortable, that's all right. I'll be here whenever you'd like to discuss whatever. I am sorry for upsetting you in the kitchen some weeks ago. My intentions were never to cause you inner pain or hurt." My head tilted to the right as my brows furrowed. A genuine fake smile spread across my lips.

"It was my fault. I'm sorry," Sarah said softly, still looking away.

"Remember what I said a few minutes ago? We can't move on if we're still living in the past. What happened, happened. It's over. Done. Forgotten."

"Really?" Slowly her irises met mine. A timid, immature nature remained rooted in her core.

Slow and steady with this one.

"Really. Now, I'd enjoy hearing more about Ms. Sarah, the elementary school teacher, if you're up to talking about it." Returning to a neutral position, I displayed tranquil posture. If I was at ease, she'd be too – the mirror effect. Due to her skittish, anxious, unwillingness to bring up her former life behavior, a simple shift to a more enjoyable topic should loosen her up enough to get inside of her cluttered mind.

She tittered. "I wasn't a nursery school teacher where the kids called me Miss Sarah. I taught third grade. They called me Mrs. Davis. Third grade is a tough year for a lot of children. Transitioning from lower elementary to intermediate elementary can be hard. I totally understood their struggles." Sarah's happiness faded and her body tensed again.

"Change sucks most times. Not a huge fan of it myself, but some of the changes I've made, not changes others have made for me, forcing me to simply accept whatever it is they wanted from me, have been good ones."

"True, but most of the things I had to learn to live with weren't because it was something I necessarily wanted." Her attitude hardened. Her usual warm, brown eyes turned icy hard.

"Care to unpack that bag for me? This is a safe space. Whatever said stays between us. Please know, I'd never, *ever* use it against you. I'm here to help, not harm. Unburden yourself, Sister Sarah. Allow me the pleasure of healing you."

With that, she did, for over three hours. After her session I realized her influence and reach within the house was tremendous. Shortly, the others requested regular sessions. One by one they all purged their pain and a therapy plan for each was put into play, immediately. Curing all of them wasn't going to be an easy fear, but in time they'd wake up and realize where they currently were was no better than where they'd come from. When that happened, I'd lead the revolt against Warren. The sick bastard wouldn't see it coming either. Revenge was mine for the taking.

Chapter 10

Jillian

The once busy home Nick and I shared rapidly evolved into a silent prison where time stood still. After viewing the news and reading far too many articles about Nick's disappearance, I had to stop or else I'd lose my mind. The things people were saying were awful, hurtful, and untrue. Even my own network reported stories without fact checking. Neighbors whom I'd never met, individuals suggesting they were close, personal friends of Nick and me were all cashing in with lies to collect their fifteen minutes of fame, but the worst was the statement made by the Winters Family. Tag, along with Miranda, Nick's siblings, and grandparents held their own press conference, passive aggressively alluding to the fact I had something to do with the abduction. They never came right out and directly said it, but subtext strongly pointed a firm finger in my direction. Tag went on endlessly about how unhappy his son was being married to me. In fact, their last conversation, which occurred right before Nick disappeared, was one filled with Nick begging his parents to help him escape my grip. Miranda went on to add that she and Tag were in the process of attempting to help him seek shelter from the storm I kept dumping on his life. In hindsight, to the discerning critic, their words of dismay, severe torture over this situation, and outright blaming me could be viewed as them having their corrupt fingers all over Nick vanishing. They made it seem a plan was concocted to place Nick in hiding, safely away from me – the Wicked Witch of the North Shore. Upon pondering it further, perhaps they were involved. Maybe the Winters family had abducted him? Somewhere on their compound Nick might be just fine, sipping whiskey, relaxing, laughing at what's been going on, and over how foolish I was for pursuing his whereabouts. But, the rational side of me, though adding Tag and Miranda to my personal list of possible suspects, was more than one hundred percent sure Nick would never, ever do such a thing. Truth be told, he loved his family, but never liked them much. However, during each presser, Beau stood far off to the left side, almost off camera with his head down, clutching his wife's hand. He appeared in a deep state of genuine distress, or was he? His stature could be a clear sign of shame. Exactly what did he know about Nick's whereabouts?

After watching that, I turned the television off and threw the remote against the wall in the living room with the force of a thousand men. While cleaning up the mess, I swore I'd stay away from and off all media, a promise I've since kept.

Initially, I hoped Jack would be able to get everyone off my ass. Issue a press statement or something. In the past, there wasn't a scandal he couldn't spin his clients' way out of with some fancy combination of words. However, this time, with the police and FBI involved, he had to keep a distance. When questioned, Jack would provide canned answers. Usually he'd either say something along the lines of me not being a suspect, or a general "no comment." He reached out a few times apologizing for not being of more assistance, but with his hands tied what was I supposed to do? Fire him? It wasn't his fault.

The FBI returned to search the house two days after the press conference, taking at least twenty large, packed boxes along with them. A dozen calls from Charles to Agent Wilder, and three weeks later, my personal effects were returned. They sat in the foyer. The desire to sort through each box, carefully returning items to their rightful place didn't exist. The shit could stay there until Doom's Day for all I cared, because no one was even an inch closer to bringing Nick home. With no work and absolutely nothing to do, a lot of pacing and internal dialogue occurred. Aside from Liam and occasionally Lyla, no one from the station reached out. Eating and sleeping held little to no interest. Those activities were time wasters, but to be honest, so was the restlessness I'd been experiencing.

Once I attempted to leave the house to return to the church to see if the police or FBI missed something, but the moment I reached the front gates, the press pounced. No sooner did they see my car, the dull voices heard from inside of my house turned into loud, booming screams of accusations. They yelled statements in the form of questions, all of which more-or-less demanded to know if I murdered Nick and where I was hiding his body. Had I decided to fight my shaking hands and keep going they would've tailed me, then the media frenzy shit storm would've followed shortly thereafter. With the landline phone not ringing as much anymore – mainly because Charles threatened any reporter who kept calling with severe legal action, I didn't need or want to tempt fate.

Don't get me wrong, I screened all correspondence, but the unnecessary harassment at all hours of the day and night finally stopped.

Fiddling with the keys on my laptop, not knowing what to do with myself, my cell beeped. My fingers quickly grabbed the device out of anxiety it might be Nick, news about Nick, and out of boredom. It was only a hair past seven in the morning and I'd already had four cups of coffee.

—Call me when you see this—Liam wrote.

Sinking into the kitchen chair, I dialed his number. Part of me experienced relief it had nothing to do with Nick, but the other part was sorely disappointed.

"Hey," I said, the second he answered. Liam reached out daily to check up on me, but hadn't come by in a while. Between the press camped outside of my house and with the station giving him other shows to produce, he had no time. Plus, he had his own things going on with his wife and kids.

"Good morning. How are you doing today? Any word on Nick?" His tone sounded more chipper than usual.

"The same and no. I would've called if anything happened." I sighed.

"I may have stumbled across something that could potentially shed some light on his whereabouts."

I sat straight up. My heart pounded. "What? What do you have? What do you know?" I spat out as fast as my lips allowed.

"I'm sure the police and FBI have investigated every angle of this case, but last night, after I finished producing your fill-in show – which, might I add, is awful and the ratings are almost at flatline status, it hit me – street cameras. Diggs, from IT, was still in his office so I asked him how one goes about getting that data. He went on and on about how only law enforcement had access to street cameras and how store owners didn't have to let anyone see them because the tapes are private property. Fast forward – a hundred dollars and that bottle of Johnny Walker Black in my office later, he showed me how to hack into them. It's rather easy, actually. I thought it'd be a lot harder. With this in mind, coupled with my newfound skill, I thought I'd swing by and we could look at the camera footage ourselves. See what we can come up with. Yes? No?"

"Yes. When?" A tremendous sense of hope filled my otherwise lifeless core. I'd foolishly been leaving everything up to the police and FBI, truly believing no stone would be left unturned. In hindsight, that was wrong. An epic failure and a bad move. Off the top of my head, I couldn't count how many times I'd interviewed people involved in cases where law enforcement had screwed up. That's not to say they always did, but it happened more times than one would believe. A simple overlook of even the smallest of clues could end up being the reason a case goes cold or the victim is never found. Why couldn't that be the issue occurring presently?

"I'm pulling up to the gates now. Raul is buzzing you."

Within seconds the security phone rang. I picked it up and instructed the guards to let Liam in. My breath caught in my throat as doubt crept into my brain. For every ounce of rational thought inside of me, there was an equal amount of reservation. What could Liam and I possibly see that the police and FBI hadn't? They were trained professionals, whereas we were only a producer and a reporter.

Stop it! You're giving up before you even begin. Nothing ventured is nothing gained. There's a good, strong chance you might observe something missed. No one is perfect, and no one in this world is always spot on at their job. Not even the FBI.

Within minutes Liam had set up his laptop on the large, square, glass coffee table in the living room. No idea why, but I shut the blinds, turned on the lights, and sat beside him on the floor. His fingers worked fast pulling up a traffic light camera positioned several feet away from the church. In silence we watched the grainy black and white footage. A little while into the feed I spotted Nick's Lexus. He turned into the parking lot, but the space was out of view. Behind him a church style van followed. The vehicle appeared light in color, but that meant nothing on CCTV. During the dead time, no one drove in or out of the lot. Cars and trucks passed the building, but not a single soul entered. Then, the van came back on the screen, but not Nick. We watched for what seemed like hours before my car appeared. Unless Nick was still inside of the church, which was doubtful because the FBI did a thorough sweep, the only way he could've left was on foot. Pulling up a map of St. Luke's, my eyes inspected the grounds. The only way onto the road was via the main parking lot. The back of the building was secured with what appeared to be a twelve-foot-high, possibly even taller, chain-link fence. The odds of Nick scaling that were slim to none, but possible if that's what he truly wanted. Behind the enclosure was a residential neighborhood. The two other sides of the church were commercial property – a strip mall to the left, and a gas station to the right. My gut nagged that whoever was in that van was who we were looking for, but I had to be more than one hundred percent sure before a positive claim was made. Having Liam hack into as many surrounding cameras as he could – even doorbell ones, my instinct was confirmed.

"The van. Whoever was driving that van has Nick, or at least knows where he is. It's the only option, because Nick's SUV didn't make a move once parked and he didn't abandon his Lexus and take off on foot either. Additionally, there's no way he's still inside of the church. We need to find that van on the video again. Let's see if the license plate is clear or if we can get a quick look at the driver."

Doing as told, Liam clicked the back button. When the target returned, he paused the feed. Grabbing a piece of scrap paper, I scribbled what I believe the plate read, but I wasn't completely positive due to the fuzziness of the image. Liam agreed he saw the same letter and number combination. Standing and reaching for my cell phone, Liam took hold of my wrist.

"What are you doing?" he asked.

"Calling Agent Wilder. Why?"

"No. You're not. What we just did is *so* illegal," Liam informed. His eyes grew wide with warning.

"Then what do you propose we do with this new found information? Nick is out there, somewhere. If they find the owner of the van, they'll find Nick." My thought process seemed logical. I wasn't sure why Liam wasn't viewing it that way.

"Jill, the cops and FBI have probably already seen this footage. It was more than likely one of the first things they looked at. What we're doing here stays between us, *unless* we happen to stumble across something extremely suspicious or see the actual kidnapping. Got it? Because if you can't agree to this, it ends now and I'm going home."

"Fine," I mumbled begrudgingly.

"Good. I'm going to call Randy. See if he can run this plate or if he knows someone who can." Liam stood, and went to the kitchen.

Several long minutes later he rejoined me. "W. Lessor. Montauk. That's who the van is registered to. I've got an address here. Randy couldn't find anything else on Lessor and neither could I with a search engine search. But, never-the-less, this is a start," he said, waving a slice of paper in the air. "Also, on the down low, he shared St. Luke's has been inspected four times. The place was picked apart. Not a crack, scratch, or speck of dust was ignored. According to the FBI's findings, Nick's fingerprints were captured on a pew and a door handle, which means he was inside of the main area at some point recent to his disappearance, but eyewitnesses – two older woman who were there that night, claim to have seen a man who resembled Nick enter and leave. They also said he was sitting beside a middle-aged man who followed Nick out. Currently, there are no suspects. The tip line the FBI is hosting averages roughly five thousand calls a day, but none of the information has proved valid."

"Let's go. What are you waiting for?" I directed, walking to the foyer, and sliding my sneakers on.

"Whoa. Slow your role. You can't just leave the house without the swarm of media vultures outside of the gates tailing you. Hell, whenever I leave they're on my ass for at least a dozen blocks before they realize I'm only going home or to work. Once they followed me into the damn grocery store. They go away, but the situation is dangerous. You want to race over to this house, I do too, but we need to be smart before doing something stupid. I'm not, and never will be, a shoot first, ask questions later kind of man."

"Then what do you propose?" I challenged. My hands firmly gripped my hips. Had I been in my right mind, I would've come up with an idea, but possessing an address where Nick might be took control over everything else.

"For starters, we need a decoy – not only to get out of here, but to not blow your cover should this Lessor guy or girl know who you are. If he or she does and sees you snooping around, we're as good as dead, because who the hell knows how much of a psycho this person is? Give me twenty minutes and I'll have a plan of attack."

With that, he exited the space and went upstairs. To where? I had no idea, but when Liam said he had a situation under control, he always did. His word was his bond.

Chapter 11

Liam

What the frigging hell did I get myself into? You're a stone's throw away from past middle age, overweight, a borderline diabetic with hypertension, high cholesterol, and off the chart triglycerides. Basically, you're one burger and donut away from a heart attack. In addition, let's not forget, you're a black man – which of course makes it a totally safe move to go snooping around, getting all up in the authorities' business. You've got a wife who, if she knew what you were up to would murder you in cold blood, and children – one of whom is on bedrest seven months pregnant, living at your house because her husband is a waste of time loser with a job that requires massive travel, making him the most useless person alive.

The weight of anxiety and stress bore down heavily on my shoulders. It's not that I didn't care for Jillian, I did and always would. I viewed her as my own child. If it wasn't for me she'd still be some local beat reporter for a crap news station, but was this current predicament really my problem? Nope. Nick was a good man. He'd been rather tolerant of Jillian and her quirky behaviors – yes, that's how I've chosen to view her obnoxious, diva-like ways. The problem with celebrities usually was their inability to take no for an answer and their tremendous egos. Jillian's ego was currently the size of the entire United States, surrounding territories included. The kid knew she was good – damn good at what she did. With her constant, insatiable desire to prove everyone around her, especially Nick's family, wrong about her worth and talent, the backing of a major network only made the wounded little girl inside of her lash out further. After Nick's indiscretion with his former assistant, Jillian changed. Though she pretended all was well, he cut her, deep. Instead of allowing the gash to scab up and heal, Jillian didn't. She kept going, faster and stronger, which in turn made her public image likability go down, but somehow her ratings rocketed through the roof.

I'd worked as a producer on many shows, but *The Bottom Line* was by far the most unique program around. A no-nonsense woman in a position of self-created power who refused to raise her voice on air, nor accept lies from guests, gave the network the boost it needed to stay afloat. Jillian always remained neutral, free of bias, despite her deep ties to the Winters.

Splashing cold water on my face, I observed my reflection in the master bathroom mirror. Dark bags. Tired eyes. Prominent frown lines. Crow's feet so deep all the creams Kendra owned combined wouldn't be able to erase them. I'd been working like a dog since this shit storm started. The toll on me was draining. At this clip I'd resemble a ninety-year-old man in less than a month. Between the Jillian/Nick fiasco and Robbins riding my ass like a racehorse he needed to win the Triple Crown, the day, month, and year, had escaped my once sharp mind. The show was in the crapper without Jillian at the helm. Didn't matter what celebrity host took over or even what guests were scheduled. No one could do the job the way she did. Robbins wanted to blame the declining ratings on Jillian's current negative media state, but deep down he knew that wasn't the case. If this nonsense didn't wrap up shortly, not only Jillian would be out of a job, we'd all be, and the station would crash hard to the bottom of the pack with a slim chance of survival. Perhaps my motives for helping her came with a healthy side of self-serving needs, but I had little responsibilities that arrived every month in the form of bills. Letting Kendra and the kids down wasn't going to happen. At my age, networks weren't interested in me or my resume. They wanted young people fresh out of college who'd work for pennies on the dollar just to get their foot in the door.

Can't do this. Nope. I'm done. This isn't my circus.

A split-second decision was made to go back downstairs and tell Jillian I was out. Yeah, she'd be pissed, but I'd be safe. There was too much to risk losing when this went south, which it would. I'd remain present, but only in an emotional capacity, on my terms. That I could handle. Not having a job, wife, home, family, or life, I couldn't rationalize. Exiting the bathroom, my pupils scanned her and Nick's room. I'd never seen it before, so of course curiosity got the better of me. The area was bright and open. A king size bed was positioned against the adjacent wall, flanked by two nightstands with tall, crystal lamps. A white-washed armoire, chest of drawers, and French dressing mirror were strategically placed around the room. A mounted flat screen television hung on the wall to the right above an electric fireplace. Curtains and linens, though snowy in appearance like the rest of the space, appeared easy and carefree. The composition was a bit shocking being the rest of the house wasn't as airy and light. Even the furniture bore a stark contrast. Pale-colored feminine wood verses the dark, heavy masculine pieces downstairs. Carefully walking across the silvery carpet to not stain it, my eyes stopped, browsing the pictures on the dresser. There, right in the front was one of her and I right before our first show.

Damn it!

The image tugged on my heartstrings. I clearly remembered that night. I doubt it would ever be forgotten. This young, talented, well-spoken, highly educated, hungry, beautiful girl was embarking upon an explosive career. I did that. I discovered, taught, and nurtured *The Bottom Line* from it's infancy. It was just as much my baby as it was hers. There we stood, many years younger. Her arms were wrapped around my waist. My head was leaning on top of hers. We were both smiling. An excitement twinkled in our faces. Better days memorialized to live on forever – especially during the difficult times, like now.

To think it all started with me breaking my leg as a result of slipping on black ice outside of the studio. Back then I was producing several shows, none of which were going anywhere. The station's ratings were at an all-time low. If a show didn't pick up, pink slips were going out, and the doors would close, permanently. I feared losing my job in such a way, sleepless nights had become a staple of my life. Kendra had just been laid off, so we needed my paycheck more than ever. While recovering at home, every morning Kendra turned on the local news. The reporters were awful and talentless. No one had any idea where to look to capture the corresponding camera angle, never mind possessing the knowledge of how to engage viewers with charm and finesse. *But* one beat girl, Jillian Winters, whom I'd met several months earlier at a book signing for her husband, consistently nailed her delivery each and every single time.

We'd chatted briefly at the event, but I dismissed the fact she said she was a journalist. In my field you meet wannabes all day. Most of the time they weren't worth a second thought because they were vultures who, when confronted with someone who could potentially boost their career, descended. Been there. Done that. Annoying as all hell. However, for Jillian it didn't matter the topic, and trust me, they'd given her the crappiest of stories to cover. She delivered information with a fierce passion. Whatever she reported on, I trusted her words. Her emotions read clear and seeped through the television. When she interviewed local residents, she'd make sure to cover a culturally diverse group, focusing on age, race, gender, and sexual orientation. Not many in her field paid much attention to small details such as that.

About two weeks later, New York was hit with a catastrophic hurricane. Guess what? There was Jillian Winters on the Jones Beach Boardwalk reporting live, tethered with a bungee cord to a lamppost as her slender body was tossed around like a plastic bag in the wind, keeping her audience updated. The only time she left post was when the eyewall approached, and it wasn't even her decision to. A rouge piece of debris flew through the air almost knocking her on her ass, causing the cameraman to grab her, insisting she get back in the van. She kept telling him to take shelter and film from the news truck, that she was totally fine, but after she almost bit the big one, he took hold of her, and carried her to safety. The girl wanted the story in the worst way.

A short while after that, she was given a seat at the anchor desk. Trust me when I tell you, she earned it. The few moments of daily banter between her and her male co-host always included her gushing over her husband. It was sweet and rather touching how much she adored him. She quickly became Long Island's local sweetheart. One would be hard pressed to not fall for her beauty, aptitude, and charm. Jillian was your classic girl next door. With each passing day, I became captivated by her ways. Her voice, eyes, and body language placed you in a trancelike state. Her laugh – infectious. Her compassion – deep rooted.

It wasn't until I saw the undercover expose she did for her old network that I was sold this was the station's solution for gaining ratings and climbing out of the bankruptcy hole. Jillian Winters crossed family party lines to uncover political corruption on Long Island. She spent months working on the project with no financial backing from her network, only a promise if the piece was good enough, they'd air it. The woman must've worked round the clock because not only did she never miss her anchor shift, but she worked as a volunteer for one of the senate candidates who was up for re-election. Jillian seamlessly changed her appearance, name, and created a new persona so nobody would know who she was. Filming with an American flag video camera pin, the final result? Twenty-five indictments for local and higher up government officials causing quite a stir in Washington. After that, I reached out to her. She interviewed with Topher and he hired her sight on scene. The rest is history.

The night of her first live broadcast, I found her pacing the set while reviewing the copy of the night's show. Racing nerves was obviously the cause, but once we sat and chatted for a bit, she calmed down saying even though this was what she'd been working her entire career for, her biggest fear wasn't screwing it up, but letting Nick down. Her political piece upset the Winters family, but Nick stood firmly by her side, defending her to them. He shielded and protected her. If she disappointed him and messed this chance up, she worried he'd be disenchanted and the pride he felt for her would vanish. I don't remember what I said to ease her worried mind, but I do remember encouraging the ideal that we were in this together, and that I'd never leave her side no matter what. She took out her cell phone and had one of the stage hands snap a quick picture of the two of us, suggesting that moment was one she never wanted to forget, even if the show went belly up. And now, the memory of that faithful night captured on film lived on her dresser, front and center, staring at me, jogging my old, tired, over-worked brain of the promise to always be in her corner – no matter what.

Damn it!

There was no way I could abandon her at such a tremendous, crucial time. Not when she needed help the most. Who else did Jillian have? Blood family? Nope – all gone. Friends? Negative. They were all fake phonies. The Winters Family? Yeah, right. I'd been watching their every move via interviews and endless press conference updates. They were waiting for precisely the right moment to hang and crucify Jillian. That girl may have been a lot of things, but when all was said and done, she loved her husband and was a good person. All the almighty, powerful Jillian Winters had was Kendra and me. She deserved her happily-ever-after. With a heavy sigh, I extracted my phone from my back pocket and placed a call.

"Hey. It's Liam. I need a favor, not for me, but rather for Jill," I said into the receiver, praying this play stood a chance in Hell.

****

An hour later, I ushered Lyla into the foyer. The plan was simple. The camped-out press knew I was inside of the house. If I left with Jillian, they'd, without a doubt, follow us. However, if they saw another woman enter the premises who they couldn't identify, they'd go to quick work to figure out exactly who she was. Once they realized it was Jillian's assistant, then saw her and I leave, they wouldn't think anything of it. The vultures would believe Lyla and I were together and Jillian remained in the house like she had been. I made sure to have Lyla dress down in a pair of gray, loose fitting yoga pants, a light pink long sleeve t-shirt, white tennis shoes, a baseball cap, and an oversized coat of her choosing. When she arrived, I pulled the same, almost identical outfit out of Jillian's closet. Jillian pulled her hair back into a ponytail, putting Lyla's hat, coat, and sunglasses on. If she moved quickly enough from the house to the car, no one would suspect the switch. I'd make quick time out of the driveway and onto the main road. Everything would be okay…maybe. Silently, I prayed to every God known.

"Stay inside of the house, away from the windows. Don't answer the phone, make any calls from your cell phone, or open any social media. Who the hell knows who's monitoring the house, and Wi-Fi traces are easy to do these days. Anyone finding out you're here in place of Jill will cause a stir, which we don't want or need at the moment, or ever, for that matter." Tension rose the closer go time neared. Clutching the keys in my hand, the metal dug into my calloused skin. Any deeper and I'd have drawn blood.

In a strong attempt to remain calm, I guided Jillian out of the garage. Holding the passenger side car door open, she slid in. Without pause, as to not draw attention to us, I acted in my best "business as usual" fashion. Sweat formed on my brow while exiting the gates. Out of the corner of my eye, Jillian appeared to be busying herself with random items in the glove box.

Well played, my little undercover reporter.

She was drawing on skills she learned years ago when building her career. A flawless actress, indeed. Merging onto the highway, I glanced in the rearview mirror. No tail. We'd done it. Made a clean break.

"We're good," I said.

Jillian's rigid body nodded curtly.

"Hey," I said, still keeping firm focus on the road. "Nick's going to be okay." Though unsure if I believed the words myself, exactly what does one say during a time like this? Your husband may or may not be dead, but chin up, buttercup. Reaching for her hand, I squeezed it.

The remainder of the ride was quiet, the only noise coming from the GPS system in the car.

"Bear right at the fork. Your destination will be on the left," the female navigator's voice spoke through the speakers.

Assessing the area, we were in the middle of nowhere. Not a single thing was around, only overrun forest. Off in the distance on the property stood a small, rundown shack. The heavy timber structure appeared to have been vacant for decades. Front window shutters hung by a thread. The roof partially was collapsed. It goes without saying the building was in dire need of a healthy dose of TLC and a good handyman.

"Are you sure this is the right place?" Jillian asked as her eyes scanned everything in sight.

"That's the address Randy gave me," I replied, double checking the paper I'd written the information down on verses the GPS coordinates.

"This can't be right."

Firing off a quick text to my brother, my brain went into overdrive surveying the area for anything out of the ordinary, such as traps or cameras. Getting out of the car and investigating on foot felt too dangerous. Waiting for Randy to confirm was the safer option. The phone beeped seconds later. This was, in fact, the correct location.

"Stick to me like glue, Jill. This place is what horror movies are born from. Keep your eyes open, mind sharp, and look alive," I warned.

Reaching into the center console, I found my trusty, old pocket knife. Clutching it tightly, I made my way out of the vehicle with Jillian close behind. Cautiously approaching the house, the wooden floor boards on the porch creaked under our combined weight. To say the experience proved unnerving would've been a gross understatement. At any given second this rickety structure could give out. Tiptoeing to the closest window, I peered in. Jillian followed suit. No one lived here. There was nothing but random, discarded, broken furniture. Thick layers of dust, cobwebs, and grime clung to every surface. However, to the left of the front door was a mailbox which clearly read, "LESSOR, W."

indicating this was his home, thusly proving Randy's intel was correct.

Slowly backing away from the house, we circled the perimeter only to find nothing but more abandoned crap. Visually cueing Jillian it was time to go, I got back in the car. My fingers poised to lock the doors immediately after Jillian got in, because my gut screamed to get the hell out of here. There was nothing of any help – not even a single, tiny breadcrumb of information to be had. Jillian started heading back to the car, but stopped abruptly. Leaning down, something caught her attention. What? No idea, but she sprinted to the car, found the tissue box on the backseat, returned to the area in question, and scooped something up. Like a trained spy, she scouted the entire space around the house again, but this time snapping pictures with her cell. Once satisfied, she joined me in the safety of the vehicle.

"Let's go," she said.

"What did you find?" I questioned, pulling back onto the road.

"Obviously, the address raises suspicions. This house isn't a primary, permanent residency, but that's not to say someone hasn't lived here full-time at some point. Based on size, décor, and location, I'd guess it's more of a summer/vacation home – a long forgotten one. There's no basement or storm cellar. It's a one-room shack. W. Lessor probably uses it to hide their true location, or as storage for miscellaneous odds and ends. All that tells me is he or she is concealing a secret. Why use this shack and not a PO Box like normal people do when they don't want anyone knowing their mailing address? What I found was somewhat fresh foot prints measuring roughly eleven inches and were noticeably wide in width. The sole of the shoe in question resembled that of a boot with a fairly distinct S-shaped marking on the bottom. Also, near the marks were newer tire tracks which may or not be from a van like the one we saw on the video, and these," she said, opening the tissue. Inside were a half dozen nails.

"Where are you going with this, Jill?" Damn this girl was good. She'd always be an investigative reporter no matter how many award-winning shows she hosted. This was her passion. It read clearly across her face. The lifelessness which once hung from every inch of her skin had been replaced with a vibrant, hopeful glow.

"The boot prints, tire tracks, and nails are all new, recently placed. Someone has been here within the past week. We had a downpour three days ago. Look around. There's practically no grass, only dirt. When dirt gets wet, it makes mud. When someone steps in mud it leaves an imprint – a cast of sorts until another rain event occurs when it gets washed away. I'm sure the cops or FBI investigated this place weeks ago, but I'm also sure if W. Lessor has a brain in his or her head, they've steered clear, aware law enforcement might come nosing around. When the police canvassed the place initially, none of these clues would've been present." She paused, attempting to read my expression.

"The boot size I came up with by comparing it against mine. I'm a size nine. The print was two inches longer and practically triple the width of my sneaker. The tire marks, I'm not familiar with cars and trucks, but I did take pictures of everything. I'll have to look stuff up when I get home. As for the nails, they're not rusty – if no one has been out here in a while, then they'd be covered in reddish brown crud. These are shiny, newish, *and* have 'J&S' stamped on the head. It's a solid place to start. After I match the shoe tread and figure out where these nails came from, I may have a lead. These are valuable clues. Granted, I would've loved to have found Nick stashed somewhere here safe and healthy, but this is progress too. I realize I'm not a cop and have never investigated an abduction, but I'm also not an idiot. What we found today is a firm start."

With a nod, I pressed the accelerator a bit harder. She was right. These were fantastic signs. Her rational thought process made sense. Law enforcement may not have been privy to this new insight. Chances were they did their initial investigation, found squat, and put a pin in it while checking out other tips. It wouldn't be the first time the police missed something or had their attention drawn elsewhere. Besides, it couldn't hurt checking Jillian's new finds out safely behind a computer screen at her house. That was much more lucid and legal than snooping around a potential whack job's abandoned home.

"Have you given any thought to what Wilder said about those two women? What were their names? Do you remember?" I asked. The thought randomly popped into my head. Truthfully, I'd forgotten about them. My central focus had been on keeping Jillian out of jail, not Nick's extra-marital bedroom conquests.

"No. I assume they're *special friends* of Nick's since the police or Wilder haven't mentioned them again. They've probably already looked into the pair," she replied. Her eyes looked straight ahead as her body turned rigid again.

"They're possible clues too, Jill. Now's not the time to get butt hurt over speculation. When we get back to the house and Lyla leaves, let's order some takeout, and dig through what we found today. I'm going to call Kendra now to tell her I'll be late. Sound good?"

"Yes. Thank you, Liam."

"Anytime, Jill. Like I always say, what are work fathers for?" I chuckled.

"Damned if I know." For the first time in weeks, she laughed. Hopefully the sentiment would sustain for longer than a few moments. After everything Jillian had endured, she deserved it. However, despite my gut suggesting we were onto something huge, my brain spun another narrative. A story which landed my ass squarely in danger.

Chapter 12

Nick

Increments of time in this shit-hole prison dragged. I'd lost track of how long I'd been here. All I knew for sure was I had to keep going. Giving up wasn't an option. What did the future hold? I hadn't a clue. There wasn't a damn thing to escape and go home to. Jillian was gone. A part of my drive, my will to carry on, to fight like hell to get out of here had crumbled. Some days I felt that staying in place and conforming to Warren's psychotic ways was the best option. Other days, I could've reached across the dinner table and strangled him in cold blood, relishing watching the life slip from his pathetic body. He'd struggle at first. His arms would wildly make feeble attempts to remove my hands from his neck, but then he'd calm. His eyes would widen as his windpipe desperately gasped for one last ounce of oxygen. Then, nothing. Silence. Freedom. Today was one of those bad moments where I danced on that fine line between sanity and pure insanity.

Warren and Noah left early in the morning to head into town to pick up supplies and food. Brother Isaac had been under the weather. According to Noah, he required an antibiotic. My suspicions he was a medical professional were confirmed when Warren shared that Noah was a Licensed Nurse Practitioner. Sickness of any kind was hardly an issue in this house. My guess is because no one went anywhere aside from the cousins, but from time to time all humans caught a random case of the sniffles, suffered from allergies, or contracted some sort of self-inflicted issue. Before taking off, Warren requested I keep an eye on things and checkup on Isaac in his absence, to which I agreed. There wasn't much to do. The "flock" had their daily routine and didn't require anyone babysitting them. Isaac was a grown man who had surely endured a variety of ailments over the course of his life at one point or another. He'd be fine. The rest were well versed in staying inside, never speaking to anyone outside the house, and not opening the front or back door unless otherwise instructed. Only Warren could do that. However, none of this was ever an issue because no one had swung by for a visit since I arrived.

I stood in the kitchen cleaning the breakfast dishes, staring out of the back window. With the exception of a few busying themselves in the den, most were in the yard tending to various chores. They'd be out there for a few hours, probably breaking for lunch later than normal. The weather shifted from warm to downright frigid. Whatever was in the ground needed to be pulled, and the rest of the gardening had to wrap up as soon as possible. Initially, my day looked like fabricating data from sessions for Warren, but with him gone a thought struck. He and Noah had internet access. If I convinced everyone to go outside, I'd accidently lock the back and basement doors, and sneak up to one of their rooms, hop online, and send an SOS message to my grandfather. Solid plan, right?

"Sisters? Brothers?" I called.

"In here," Brother Richard replied.

Going into the front sitting room, I found four of them folding wash.

"Listen, the weather is turning brutally cold. There's a lot of work to be done outside. Wouldn't it be a great surprise for Brother Warren if when he got home all of the yard work was complete? If there's extra time, I thought we could take it even further and start jarring the remaining produce. I'll keep an ear out for Brother Isaac and tend to his needs," I said, leaning against the wall, and smiling brightly at these severely damaged souls. The more I got to know them in session, the more my heart wept. The pain, abuse, and neglect they'd all come from before here was unspeakable. Slowly, I gained their trust. Our meetings went smoothly. Little by little without their knowledge I was helping them along the healing path. One day in the near future they'd be strong enough to realize how wrong this setup was. When that happened, I'd be ready to lead them to freedom. After that, I'd assist them in finding the help they'd require to function in the real world.

"What a wonderful idea," Nicole exclaimed. Her story was by far the worst to date. Not only was she abused physically and mentally by her parents growing up, but her husband had done the same. The others nodded in agreement.

"Brother Warren asked I tend to a few things around the house, then I'll meet everyone outside. I shouldn't be any more than an hour or so. We can worry about the wash later," I explained.

Like lambs to the slaughter they rose, grabbed their coats, and exited the house. No questions. No replies. Nothing. I couldn't help but feel bad for these people.

Not wanting to waste any time, I scaled the stairs two by two to Warren's room. The damn door was locked. Picking it was beyond my skill set. That was more of a Jillian thing – my Nancy Drew. Heading three doors down to Noah's space, his knob clicked open.

The space was sparse and rather tidy. He had few personal items. The walls were bare, free from art or family photographs. On an oak desk was a small picture of a young girl. Had I not been in such a rush, I'd have studied the image more. From the quick glance taken, she had long, dark ashen, beachy waves, with sparkling green eyes, and smooth rosy skin. She couldn't have been any more than twenty-five. However, the thought of this pretty girl standing next to him didn't match-up. His large face, empty, hollow eyes, with a mess of dark brown out of control curls when it grew too long didn't mesh with the beautiful woman from the snapshot. To sum it up best, she was a fine wine one drank from an expensive crystal flute. He was a cheap can of beer you'd drink from a brown paper bag behind a convenience store.

Luck appeared to be on my side when I moved the mouse to the desktop around a bit. The screen flashed on; icons popped up. No password was required. Clicking on the first internet app I spotted, images loaded. Feverishly, I typed "Jillian Winters." Millions of hits came up, but none of them mentioned her passing.

Odd.

Hitting the "news" tab, the first article that appeared was about how she'd been hiding out in our house since the press conference she held two weeks after my disappearance. The police and FBI were involved, investigating all possible angles. A little farther down was a picture the paparazzi took stamped two days ago of a grainy Jillian inside of our kitchen.

"She's not dead," I gasped. That sick bastard lied. He made up a story to get me to stop resisting life on his crazy ass compound.

Pressing the control H key combination to delete my search, it revealed Noah had been investigating Jillian himself, and quite frequently. Looking further down the list I caught a glimpse of my name, but the sound of feet against the hardwood floors climbing the stairs sent my fingers into overdrive. After erasing my research, I bolted from the room to find Sarah reaching the top step.

"What are you doing up here?" she asked.

"I heard dripping water when I passed the stairs. It wasn't coming from the kitchen or first floor bathroom. I thought it might be from an upstairs pipe. It was. Brother Warren or Brother Noah must not have turned the sink all the way off in their bathroom before they left," I lied.

"Really? I've been by the steps a bunch of times this morning and didn't hear anything," she challenged.

"Why else would I be up here then?"

"I don't know," she answered. Behind her brown eyes rested too much suspicion. I couldn't risk her telling Warren about this. The last time Sarah and I had a run in, he concocted a story about Jillian dying. If I caused a stir again in his delicate little ecosystem, he might actually go through with harming my wife, and that wasn't about to happen.

Taking a calculated risk, I took her by the waist, pressed her body against the wall, and kissed her. She'd either accept the gesture or would scream. Thankfully, after a stunned pause, her lips moved while her arms coiled around my neck. Her fingernails gently scratched against my scalp.

"I shouldn't have done that. It was disrespectful," I said while pulling away in an attempt to flush out the situation going on inside of her head.

"Shut up," she answered as she yanked my frame back against hers.

Ready to quickly figure out a way to end what I started before it got out of control, I heard the front door lock click open. It had to be Warren and Noah home early from their errands.

Shit!

Tugging Sarah's hips into mine, I crushed my lips on hers. She met the action without objection. My brain went into shutdown because if I allowed myself to think too much over what was happening, what I was doing, I'd become consumed with guilt, regret, and remorse. This was cheating, and no matter how it was justified it would never be right. I swore not only to Jillian, but to myself, after the Kelly incident I'd never relive the same mistake again. Ever.

Stop! You have no other choice right now. You didn't elect to do this like you did with Kelly. You're being forced into this awful act, which, might I add, is what's going to keep you and Jillian alive.

Keeping Sarah's body against mine was easy. She wasn't going anywhere. Her fantasies had finally become a reality. While Sarah enjoyed the moment, my mind schemed and plotted. I didn't want this to appear to be an act of lust, but rather one of romantic interest. When Warren or Noah discovered us, I didn't need a lecture on how lust was a sin. Love on the other hand, they couldn't say a damn thing about. Sliding one arm firmly around her waist, my left hand softly caressed the side of her face. I kept the tempo of movement slow and deep, never allowing our bodies to part. Initially, she went with the flow, but after a moment she became sexually aggressive, clawing at me like a lion in heat, jerking at the waist of my slacks.

"Slow down, Sarah. I'm not like that," I whispered, retreating slightly to allow my warm breath to tease her lips.

"Nick," she moaned before slamming her lips back on mine. Her referring to me as "Nick," not Brother Nicholas, was a good, strong sign. It meant she felt vulnerable and comfortable around me, which worked to my advantage in every conceivable way.

"Ah hem," Warren coughed, alerting us to his presence.

Swiftly pivoting, I turned to block Sarah – a sneaky way to allow her to believe I was protecting her from the sudden startle.

"Brother Warren," I said, still retaining the position.

"I'm not interrupting anything? *Am I*? Is there something we *need* to discuss here?" he questioned. Though his body language remained calm, something in his eyes appeared off. I couldn't decipher exactly what.

Before I could utter a single sound, Sarah pushed past Warren and bolted down the stairs. Less than a minute later, the sound of the basement door opening and slamming shut cut through the still air.

"I have to go after her, Brother Warren. You can lecture me later on the dos and don'ts of this house, but presently I have to be there for Sister Sarah. She needs me. Sorry," I said rapidly, hoping the distracted, rushed, choppy delivery of words revealed a concerned man.

Upon entering the main space of the basement, something odd happened inside of my core. Everything emotionally driven powered down. Perhaps this is what psychopaths experienced, I had no idea, because I'd never operated in a manner as such, but the situation appeared clearer than it had minutes ago. I could now go through with this farce with a free conscience.

"Sister Sarah?" I called. Not seeing her, I assumed she was in the bathroom.

"What?" she answered, cracking the door open an inch.

"Come out and talk to me. Please," I requested, sitting on the foot of her bed.

"No."

"I won't force you to do anything you don't feel comfortable with, but I'd really like it if we could speak." I played on her weakness – kindness. A dick move, but desperate times and all that crap.

"Brother Warren is going to be mad at me," she wept.

"I'll speak with him. It will be okay. I promise, but you're going to have to trust me," I assured.

"What will you say?" She poked her head out. Traces of hopefulness seeped into her voice.

"Well, the truth. That we share feelings for each other. What he saw was an expression of those emotions." *More-or-less, I'll lie my ass off.*

"You have feelings for me?" she asked meekly, coming out a little more, but still clutching the doorknob.

"I wouldn't have kissed you if I didn't feel something." The statement was not a complete fib. Internal sentiments for her existed, just not romantic ones.

"Oh, Nick," she cooed. With swift motion she leapt into my arms.

I held her tightly, but it wasn't enough to satisfy Sarah's lust. Obviously, this woman's physical requirements knew no boundaries because self-control ceased to exist. Recapturing recent intimacies appeared to be the only thing on her mind. Her long fingernails ran up and down my spine as her teeth lightly nipping at my neck. A split-second decision had to be made. Push her away or sleep with her. Committing the sinful act would sate her sex drive, get her off my ass, and return her to a somewhat calmer state. However, both choices came with pros and cons. In the end, having Sarah on my side, manipulating her to place all of her trust and faith in me would lead to the others following suit, drawing them away from Warren and toward healthy, lasting, freedom.

Breathing deeply, my hands found and cupped her face. With every kiss, touch, sigh, and release all I thought about was Jillian and how amazing it was going to be when I saw her again. My heart and soul wanted to feel anger over being duped by Warren, but the knowledge that my beautiful wife was still in existence superseded any negativity. There was someone to return home to. Someone to fight like hell for. A reason to get out of here was waiting for me on the other side. All lost hope returned. My strength deepened. My drive was repaired. Between Jillian's stubbornness and my rooted desire to find a way back to civilization, we'd be reunited in no time.

I'm so sorry, Jill. This means nothing. She means nothing. Please forgive my indiscretion.

Chapter 13

Jillian

It's not that I wasn't grateful for all of Lyla's help, but if I could've shoved her out of the door the moment my feet stepped inside of the house, I totally would've. I had no time or desire for idle chit-chat. She had to leave so I could get to work, immediately. After exchanging a few brief pleasantries, assuring her everything was all right, I went straight to my laptop. Liam's job was figuring out who Paris Rosen and Shelly Rockland were. My focus zeroed in on boot patterns and the "J&S" stamped nails. At first glance, research went slow. There were hundreds of men's boots with similar tread patterns. My eyes grew tired and weary constantly looking back and forth between a cell phone picture and a computer screen.

An hour passed with nothing to show for it, which infuriated me. Liam appeared heavily focused on whatever was on his screen. His fingers flew over the keyboard like a madman. I resented him right then and there. As a woman who made her bones as an investigative journalist, figuring out two simple clues and how they linked back to one lunatic should've been as easy as pie. Not so much. Perhaps I'd grown lazy, rusty due to the years separating drive and desire to achieve journalistic greatness. All I really did was scan newspapers and sit on my ass nightly reading a teleprompter while interviewing the flavor of the week. Of course, I had input and inserted my own personal spin on the show often, but it was cushy. No thinking required.

"You can relax, Jill. Neither Rockman or Rosen are doing Nick, unless he's got a granny fetish," Liam said, standing in the kitchen.

Relief sprinkled over my brain, but it wasn't enough to amount to anything worthwhile. Even if the two women were sleeping with my husband, why would it matter? Quite possibly they might've been involved or perhaps a significant other of theirs went off the rails after finding out about the affair, but my gut shouted this was more than that. Joining him, I peered over his shoulder to gain full view of the screen.

"Shelly Rockman is a ghostwriter for celebrities, more specifically, politicians. Paris Rosen is her assistant. Both use fake names to conceal their true identities. In reality Shelly is Sheila Glass, and Paris is Jenna Stein. Apparently, all these 'A-List' idiots want their fans to think they wrote their tell-all books by themselves, but when put up or shut up time comes, they can't string two words together to save their lives. Enter the Rockman/Rosen team who work behind the scenes to make the *New York Times Best Sellers List* happen. How does this tie into Nick? The two women were commissioned by Beau Winters to assist in penning his autobiography. It's being released late spring; in case you'd like to pre-order a copy for some light summer beach reading. Being Nick is a Winters, one can safely assume they've been in contact to extract details from his point of view. Perhaps be privy to a fun-loving grandpa/grandson story or to get a quote. Nick is close with Beau. Makes sense. It took a little digging, but here they are," he said.

Two older women, one with short gray hair and the other with a blonde bob stood beside Beau Winters at a charity event last year – one Nick and I weren't invited to, but every other Winters had been.

"I can keep digging into them, but I feel it's a waste of time. They're a dead end. You find anything worthwhile?" Liam asked.

"No. Damn it," I hissed, slamming the palm of my right hand against the countertop.

"Nothing on the markings on the nail?" Much like myself, Liam sounded shocked over my lack of progress.

"Not a frigging thing." My head shook as internal anger thundered.

Walking into the den, Liam put on a discarded pair of rubber gloves. His thick fingers stretched in dark blue latex toyed with the nails. Moving to a nearby lamp, his eyes squinted while the light cast shadows on the objects in question.

"These are custom created. The metal color isn't consistent throughout the body. If you compare it to the other ones, they're all different. The stamp on the head was created by a cheap laser drill anyone could purchase online," Liam assessed.

As if the moon and stars aligned in one twist of fate, an epiphany struck. Racing to the computer I went straight to a popular online buy/sell auction site. Typing in the details, boom went the dynamite. J&S stood for Jamison and Sons Hardware – an East End, Long Island based mom and pop hardware store. Unfortunately, they had no website or online presence, but they did have a storefront. Upon further investigation, this shop carried a wide variety of typical goods and household construction items, specializing in hard-to-find merchandise. Their homemade screws, bolts, nuts, and nails were in demand, receiving hundreds of five-star reviews, all of which suggested the inexpensive products held up better than the popular brand names. A quick White Page search later, an address and phone number were secured. The shop wasn't too terribly far from where we'd been earlier. What sealed the deal was their large selection of work boots – all bearing the exact same tread print as the one discovered earlier. The shoes weren't made by Jamison and Sons Hardware, but rather by another local vender and sold exclusively through the store. Showing this information to Liam, a solid plan was constructed for Lyla to return to the house bright and early, and for us to take a ride to the shop. For the first time since Nick vanished I slept, hard and soundly. I was closing in on finding him, but what state he'd be in once found frightened me. I couldn't think about that now. I had to have faith and hope he was still alive and well. If "W. Lessor" laid one finger on him, he'd pay, and dearly.

****

Before the sun rose, Lyla returned, and Liam and I were off. Shockingly enough only two media trucks were camped outside of the house and both paid no attention to the movement in and out of the driveway. With no traffic and Liam putting the pedal to the metal, the typical nearly two-hour trip turned into a fifty-five-minute drive. At first a calmness existed inside of me, but the closer we got a nervous, anxious energy grew, coming to a head as he pulled off the road and into a dirt parking lot. The sound of the steel cowbell over the front door caused all rational thoughts to stop, inciting panic in a way I never experienced before. My hands trembled. My knees shook. A hot creeping sensation slowly climbed my spine, resting at the base of my tense neck.

"Pull it together, Jill. If I can clearly see you're stressed out, whoever is in here will, and may use it against you. Be cool," Liam urged once we were inside.

He was right. A metaphorical refocusing of the lens had to happen instantly. Remain sharp. Retain as much information as possible. Take mental notes on everything. The store was small, but donned a well-kept exterior. It resembled the quintessential small-town country store you'd see in movies. Aside from farmland, off in the distance homes sat on parcels of property, but grocery stores, strip malls, convenience stores, even gas stations didn't exist. This store stood alone.

Clutching the baggie with the nails in it, I moved away from the doorframe and into the main area. A sharp chill shot up my spine, causing my body to involuntarily jolt. In a rather fatherly fashion Liam pulled the front of my coat tighter around my waist and placed an arm around my shoulders. His gesture was comforting, especially on this chilly, almost subzero temperature morning.

"Let me do the talking, Jill," he said, leaning closer to my ear.

With my nod, my eyes explored the store. It was organized, but packed with merchandise. Every inch of the space was piled high with various odds and ends. The narrow aisles only allowed for one person to move at a time, suggesting not much foot traffic occurred at once. The smell of sawdust and cigars filled my nose, causing a rapid succession of sneezes.

"Bless you," an older man said, coming out of a back room. His appearance was classic, with dark blue jeans, tan shoes, and a red buffalo plaid flannel shirt. Thick white hair covered his head. Sparkling, warm blue eyes matched the smile on his face. "Can I help you folks?"

"Thank you," I replied, shooting a look at Liam. If he wanted to be the one to speak, it was now or never, or else I'd start.

"I sure hope so." Liam grinned at the gentleman. "My colleague and I stumbled across these nails and were wondering if this was the shop to buy more from."

I approached, handing him the bag. Taking a pair of reading glasses out of his breast pocket, he put them on, and examined the contents.

"You've come to the right place. These are definitely ours. Do you need a specific kind? Amount?"

"No, but thank you. Do you sell a lot of these?" Liam inquired.

"I do. A few years ago my sons came up with this idea to take scrap metal and melt it down to make nails, screws, fasteners, nuts, bolts, and things of the such. Since we have the ability to do that right here in the store, it costs us next to nothing. My sons package the items and sell them on the computer for cheaper than the big box stores do. It's a fantastic addition to the business. The oldest is creating a website for the internet. The youngest has been trying to get merchandise on shelves in larger chains and handles all of the advertising. I'm an old man. All I know is this store, which I inherited from my father, who inherited it from his. My boys want to expand – they want more. Who am I to stop them from keeping the family legacy alive while finding creative ways to make an extra buck? If they don't grow the business, one of these large corporations will eventually crush us. To see that happen would kill me."

"That's wonderful. I only hope my children will surpass my success one day like yours have been doing," Liam said. "I have another question. I saw online you sell work boots made by a local resident. Can you show me where they are?"

"Of course. Right this way. Some of the best shoes you'll ever find. Strong, tough, long lasting, all terrain and weather. Much better than the junk malls sell. These are crafted with real leather, not with a rubber/plastic composite you see on shelves today. True craftsmanship. They cost about the same, but you'll wear them twice as long. I've had this pair for five years and not a scratch. Looks like I just took them out of the box this morning."

Taking hold of the display shoes, we scanned the soles. Bingo. Shoe number three was the winner with the exact same pattern.

"These are them. I'm dead sure," I said to Liam.

"I'm going to level with you, sir," Liam started.

"Jamison. Sir and Mr. Whitlock is my father," the old man corrected.

"I'm going to level with you, Jamison. My name is Liam Stevens, and this is Jillian Winters. Jillian is the host of a nightly news program. Her husband, Nick Winters, the psychotherapist, was abducted recently," Liam informed.

"I've seen the story in the papers. I'm not much of a television watcher, so I am unfamiliar with Mrs. Winters program, but my wife has a book or two of Mr. Winters somewhere on the bookshelf at the house. I can go home and find them if that helps, otherwise I'm unsure how I can be of assistance."

"My husband is missing. I need to find him. These nails and those boot prints were found yesterday outside of this run-down shack about twenty minutes from here in Montauk. The mailbox read 'Lessor, W.' I have no idea who that is, but whoever he or she is, they drive a church style van and I'm confident they have Nick. The police and FBI have been an epic waste of time. They've more than likely investigated the shack and have encountered the same dead ends as us. If you know anything about this Lessor person, please, I beg you, tell us," I said. A tragic sense of urgency hung from each word.

"W. Lessor with these boots, those nails, and a van like you described would be Warren Lessor. The shack you're talking about was owned by his father, Wilbur. He died about twenty or so years ago. I hate to speak poorly of the deceased, but he was a real nasty man. Warren and his cousin, Noah, are frequently in here buying all sorts of odds and ends. In fact, see that pile over there?" he asked, pointing to an area on the opposite side of the store. "That's for them. They ordered it last week. Just came in. Warren said he'd be back this Friday to pick it up. Got a bunch of other things out back for him to come and grab too. He owns a nice chunk of land about fifteen minutes up the road. Big, white house with a porch. You can't miss it. Look for the mailbox with the goose and gander on it if you're unsure. I don't have a phone number because I don't think they have a landline. I can't remember if I've ever seen them with a cell phone either. Odd men, but polite and always pay their tab on time. Do you really think Warren or Noah had anything to do with your husband's disappearance?" Jamison asked, taking a step back and leaning against the front counter.

"If they didn't take him, then they know who did," I answered, thrilled over the wealth of knowledge this man provided in mere seconds. This was it. A strong sense of certainty we were actually onto something that would provide a means to an end surged inside of me.

"Is there anything else you can tell us about Warren or Noah?" Liam inquired.

"Like I said, they're decent, quiet people. I've never seen them with a woman or anyone else besides each other – neither wears a ring, nor has spoken about a significant other. They pull up in the van like the one you described every few weeks, usually around midmorning, come in, shop, and if they can't find something, they'll ask me to order it. They have a tab started by Wilbur years and years ago, but unlike him, they don't use it – always pay with cash. Depending on how busy I am, I'll help them load up. If they special order items I'll tell them when I know for sure they'll arrive so they don't waste a trip. Warren does all of the talking. Noah is silent. He stands behind his cousin with his head down. He may be slow or have special needs. Not sure. Warren's been coming in here with his father since he was knee high to a grasshopper's behind. Haven't seen any other family members. Wilbur mentioned a wife who'd passed away. I assume that was Warren's mother. Never saw him with any other children beside Warren, but that doesn't mean anything. After Wilbur died, Warren mentioned he purchased the lot down the road. That's when Noah started coming around. The two have been fixing it up little by little. They've been doing an excellent job. Place looks fantastic. Other than that, I don't know much else."

"Thank you. You've been extremely helpful. I need one last thing though. If Warren, Noah, or anyone else comes in here, you never saw us," Liam said.

"Am I or my family in danger?" Jamison's expression reflected worry. If thoughts could speak, his would be cursing him for opening the store this morning.

"No. If Warren and Noah have been coming here for years and never caused any trouble, they wouldn't start now. We don't know for certain if they have anything to do with the disappearance, it's simply a lead we're following." Liam paused. "Imagine being in Jillian's shoes. Your wife goes missing. The authorities are doing next to nothing to help find her. What would you do, Jamison?"

The elderly store owner's eyes reflected deep sympathy and sorrow. "Good luck to you both. If I can be of any more assistance, let me know."

"Thank you," I said, placing my hand on top of his and giving it a squeeze.

"They'll be here tomorrow, probably between nine and nine-thirty in the morning. When there are big orders like this, both show up. Chances are they'll want winter items too. The forecast is calling for the first snow of the season tomorrow afternoon and this old man's knees can confirm that. It's going to be a big one. I can stall them if you want to check out the house. Here's the store's number. Call if you need anything at all. As far as I'm concerned no one was here today," he said, scribbling on a slip of receipt paper he pulled from the old fashion register.

Accepting the paper, Liam shook his hand, thanking him. Back in the car, I turned to face him.

"We're both aware I'll be returning tomorrow, but you don't have to come back, Liam. I've already asked too much of you as it is. You've got Kendra, the kids, and yourself to worry about. Truth-be-told, you don't need this drama. I'm capable of finishing by myself."

He'd put his neck on the line enough for me over the years, and even more so currently. I wasn't an idiot. He had a family who were far more important than me and this mess. If anything happened to him because of me, I'd never forgive myself. Years ago when faced with uncovering the shady politicians, I went in alone. This would be no different. Nick's wellbeing was at stake and I'd be damned if I didn't see this through. Liam didn't respond. Instead, he picked up his cell phone and made a call.

"Mr. Robbins, this is Liam Stevens. How are you?"

He paused while Topher spoke. I could hear the weasel's voice babble through the receiver.

"That's fantastic news. I'm happy I was able to boost their ratings. Listen, I have a family emergency and won't be able to make it in tonight or tomorrow while Kendra and I deal with it. Put Gregory Cage in my place. I trained the kid. I'm confident he'll do the same as I would and will crush it."

More chatter.

"I don't know, Mr. Robbins, which is why my wife and I need to attend to this personal matter."

Fully expecting to hear screaming from Topher's end, I heard nothing.

"Thank you, sir. I appreciate it. See you Monday." With that he hung up. Staring me straight in the eyes, he spoke again. "There's no way in hell I'm going to let you do this on your own. We started this together and we will end it the same way. It doesn't matter that I didn't create you, Jill. You're still one of my and Kendra's kids. Got it?"

His words caused a lump to form in my throat. I hadn't felt this secure in a long time. Since the passing of my parents and the downfall with Nick, I often felt alone and abandoned, even when I was in a room surrounded by people. A tear rolled down my cheek as a feeble, "Thank you," was whispered.

Choked up by his own emotions, he cleared this throat. "You're the undercover investigator here. What's our next move?"

"Shockingly enough it's kind of an easy one," I said as a slight optimistic smile grew on my lips. In less than twenty-four hours, by the grace of God, Nick would be home and this nightmare would end.

Chapter 14

Nick

Since spinning the epic tale of how I'd fallen for Sarah and she for me, Warren joyfully accepted the coupling, promptly moving us into a room of our own on the forbidden second floor. Explaining this wasn't what I was ready for fell on deaf ears. He kept insisting this was a blessing from God so Sarah and I could bear children for our group family. Sarah was all for it, but the thought of creating life with this woman didn't sit well. Often, I'd stay awake until the early hours of the morning suggesting I was working on log books for Warren regarding the sessions conducted or I'd head up early and pretend to be asleep when Sarah came to bed. If backed into a corner, I'd lay beside her and make up stories about my past, expressing how moving slowly was most comfortable for me due to lingering pain, to which she begrudgingly agreed. However, some nights she acted like an animal in heat. Those days were difficult to avoid. With the exception of a handful of times, satisfying her urges, then telling her that's all that mattered – her pleasure, did the trick. The few evenings when I had no other choice but to sleep with her, I'd pretend to climax. You'd think this would be the worst part of the hell I single-handedly created, but it wasn't. Sarah's insane, irrational jealousy took the prize.

When I'd conduct sessions with the other females in the house, she'd stalk by the closed door, lending an ear to make sure nothing sexual was going on – trust me, it wasn't. If I helped, spoke to, did chores with, or basically was in the same room where women were present, she'd practically lose her damn mind. She'd storm out of the space, yelling, screaming, and stomping her feet. Being I was aware of her psychological state, I was always able to calm her and provide reassurances that my loyalty remained strong for only her, but her childlike behaviors didn't stop. On Jillian's worst day she'd never been this bad.

"I have to see some of our sisters today, Sarah. You cannot spy on my sessions, nor stand outside of the door, and must remind yourself whenever you feel the urge to explode, nothing is going on between me and anyone in this house. Should you feel threatened, worried, or scared, take a few deep, cleansing breaths. Count, hold, and exhale the way I showed you," I requested while dressing.

"Yes. Anything for you," she cooed, still in bed.

"Please, Sarah. I have a lot of work to accomplish today. Every interruption is a setback, and every setback is less time for us to spend together." With a smile and a wink, I headed down the stairs to the kitchen.

"Good morning, Brother Nicholas. Brother Noah and I will be heading into town in a few minutes to pick up the supplies we ordered and a few random items for the storm coming in later," Warren informed. "Would you mind keeping an active eye on things around here in our absence?"

"Of course, Brother Warren. While you're gone I'll have a group go out back and pre-treat the walkways.

The rest can bring in wood for the fireplaces, get extra blankets on the beds, and start prepping meals for the day. I'll go out front, alone, and salt the porch and a path to the mailbox. When you return, I must begin sessions."

"Thank you, Brother Nicholas. You're a godsend. We'll try not to be too terribly long."

"Take your time. Sister Ruth said she feels a blizzard coming in her joints. You may want to stop by the market and grab some extra food, just in case."

"We planned on it."

Noah lumbered into the kitchen in his typical lowered head, shoulders slumped, eyes firmly focused on the ground avoiding all social or emotional contact, fashion. Everyone in the house except him attended sessions. He refused. I couldn't decide if he didn't want to speak with me or if Warren wouldn't allow it. Even though based off impressions he required the most therapeutic support, I didn't push because I didn't need him to stage the revolt against Warren. I'd have liked to have had an opportunity to help him, but I wasn't about to force the issue. Who the hell knew what might pop out of Pandora's Box? Too risky.

"Be safe," I said as the two men walked out of the front door.

The "flock" weaved in and out of the first-floor rooms while I sat at the table sipping coffee. Wind whipped against the side of the house, causing branches to scratch against the glass windows. The sky was eerie and gray. Alone with my thoughts, attempts to figure out what happened next developed. All I came up with was none of these people were even remotely close to believing the truth, that Warren Lessor was no savior, but rather a psychopath. I'd dug such a deep grave with him and now Sarah, it was anyone's guess how long I'd be stuck here plotting my escape. Being I slept upstairs, several attempts to enter Warren or Noah's room failed. The damn doors were always locked. A defeated depression seeped into my soul. This was it. This was my new life. I'd end up having to marry Sarah in some sort of whacked out ceremony hosted by Warren and his weirdo cousin and made to breed, creating more mentally unstable individuals for this cult. Silver lining – the marriage wouldn't be legal by any stretch of the imagination due to a lack of an official state sanctioned license, and the tiny fact I was forced into this already married. The men and women brought here by Warren were good people, damaged, but they possessed strong moral compasses. Each one held a secret story which slowly unraveled during sessions. I could help them, this was never called into question, but there were days where I felt all of this work was stupid and foolish. Perhaps this place of ignorance and avoidance each of them lived in was best. What was the point of anything anymore? If Warren's "flock" wanted this life, why would I screw that up for them? Once freed and introduced back into society – if that day ever came, would they be okay or would they be messed up beyond belief?

It's all right to be tired. It's fine to be done. It's not a sign of weakness to want out. Life is never without choices, though. You may not like the ones available, but never-the-less they are very much so present. If you decide to run out that door, there's a chance Warren will find and kill you or Jill. That's not an option. If you stay, you'll probably never leave.

Out of the corner of my eye I saw a bottle of bleach.

One cupful and I'd be dead. For the first time in my life I wrestled with suicidal thoughts. Death was the only way out. I had faith in Jillian, but that confidence had dwindled. By now I was sure she'd have figured everything out, but she hadn't. Maybe she stopped trying. Maybe she saw this as a blessing – freedom from an awful, phony existence. Was there really anything out there for me on the other side of that door?

You know there isn't. Stop lying to yourself.

"It's time," I whispered, running my hands up and down my face aggressively. Rising and moving to the plastic bottle, I lifted it off of the floor. After unscrewing the cap I paused, waiting for the rational side of my brain to kick on, begging me to stop this, to keep fighting, but it never came. All I heard was, *"This is the only way out."* Steady hands tilted the liquid to my lips. The fumes burned my nostrils. My eyes stung. One swallow later and I'd be at peace.

"I'm so sorry, Jill," I mumbled, before a sudden sound ceased the action. I heard metal scrapping by the back door lock. With none of the "flock" outside, they were either in the basement or doing chores in the family room, and Sarah was still lounging in bed, I put the bleach down, and strained my ears to hear more. The lock clicked open and the light tapping of feet against the floor sliced through the silence. My body snapped into fight mode taking hold of a chef's knife which was lying on the counter. Clutching it tightly, my knuckles turning white from the firm grip, I flattened my back against the wall, waiting for whoever dared to enter this insane asylum to make a move.

Chapter 15

Jillian

The moment Liam dropped me off at my house, I placed a call to Lyla.

"Hey, Jill. What's up?" she asked cheerily.

"I need one last favor," I said.

"Anything. Shoot."

"This stays between us, Lyla," I warned.

"That goes without saying, Jill. I haven't said anything to anyone, my fiancée included in that, about babysitting your home and pretending to be you while you and Liam went out. If you think I'd betray your trust now, then you really don't know me, and when you return to work you need to find a new assistant," she challenged.

"You're right. I'm sorry. It's been a rough ride, but that's no excuse."

"Forget about it. How can I help?" Lyla's chipper nature was what caused me to hire her in the first place. Her qualifications were subpar, this was her first swing at the assistant bat, but she proved herself to be a valuable team member in short order. She was always ready, willing, and able. Besides, everyone has to start somewhere.

I spent the next several minutes vaguely filling her in on what had been going on. Not wanting to give too much away because I wasn't sure if anyone had tapped my phones or had positioned listening devices around the house, I had one simple request. Tomorrow morning starting at nine, hawk my social media. When a live feed came up, get anyone possible on all platforms to share the hell out of the feed, and to call Agent Timothy Wilder at the FBI. With tremendous apprehension, she agreed. Sleep eluded me, so I spent the overnight hours mentally preparing by creating checklist after checklist. By the time Liam showed up, I was ready to go. Thankfully, not one single news van was parked outside of the front gates. The ride out east was long and tedious. My nerves were caught somewhere between fierceness and fearfulness.

We pulled into Jamison's lot before the sun rose. He saw us from the front window and invited us in to keep warm and for a cup of coffee. With no desire to, Liam urged we did, saying the distraction was necessary to calm my mental strain and to pass time. While the two men chatted about their children, wives, and lives, I paced the aisles, restless to get over to Lessor's house sooner rather than later, while toying with the American Flag camera pin I tacked to my coat's collar. The device was from my beat reporter days so I could catch everything I witnessed while taking down Nassau County's dirty politicians. When eight-twenty rolled around, I approached Liam.

"What's the best way to get to Lessor's home from here? The GPS says it's a straight run, but if you know a better route, I'm all ears," Liam questioned Jamison.

Glancing at map on Liam's cell phone, Jamison replied. "There really aren't any safe side streets around here. You'd be going off-road. Even in that Subaru you've got out there, if the storm should pull in earlier, you'll get lost or stuck. I suggest heading east out of here, but stopping about a half a mile before the house. There's this huge, overgrown, bunch of trees, shrubs, weeds, and sticks off to the right. The kids around here hide in there to drink, smoke, or make out. Back into the mess, kill the car lights, and wait. You'll have a clear view of the road. Warren's van is tan – only one around here. Spotting it shouldn't be an issue. When he drives by, wait two, three minutes, then pull out. Keep going east and you'll see his house on the left. There's a goose and gander mailbox right out front. You can't miss it. There's no gate or anything like that. Drive right up the gravel path."

"Thank you," Liam said, smiling warmly and shaking Jamison's hand.

"Good luck, Liam. I'll text you when he gets here and again once he leaves. I hope you find your husband alive and well, Miss. You have my number. Call if you need anything, anything at all."

With a nod we left, following Jamison's directions to the letter. As promised, a cluttered heap of greenery came into focus. Backing up using the guidance of a deep set of tire tracks, we sat, waiting, but not for long. Roughly ten minutes later, Lessor's tan, church style van rolled down the road. Two men were in the vehicle.

Nerves ran high for both Liam and I as we approached the home. Turning onto the driveway a breath caught in my throat. It was do or die time. No mistakes were allowed.

"Listen, Jill. I don't know what we're going to find in this house, but you have to be prepared and ready for whatever. Nick might be inside. He might not. Other people could be in there too. I have no idea. It quite possibly is a house of freaking horrors. Once we get inside, start rolling. Lyla will take care of the getting the FBI out here. We stick together. Don't you dare leave my line of sight. We have to hold on and stay alive just until the authorities get their asses here. The closest precinct is about fifteen minutes away. They'll be dispatched first. Ready?"

"Yeah." Calling upon Nick's advice pertaining to anxious situations, I took a series of several deep breaths through my nostrils, holding the air in for a few seconds, then exhaling through my mouth. My headspace had to empty, had to free itself from the magnitude of the situation so I could do this, and do it well. Nick's life depended on it.

"Back door," Liam instructed.

The rear lock was a simple deadbolt. I'd picked a ton of these back in the day. Extracting a bobby pin from my ponytail, I went to quick work on the tumbler. Liam surveyed the windows not seeing a soul inside. The catch clicked, and the door opened. Liam entered first, grasping a pocketknife. Pressing the back of the lapel pin, a dim red light indicated I was streaming across all social media platforms. Between Lyla blasting the feed and my over one million followers, a slight sense of peace found its way inside of my crazed brain. Cautiously, we made our way into what appeared to be the kitchen.

My breathing was shallow. My windpipe felt strangled. My hands shook, in spite of the mental warning to cut the crap and to get my head in the game – that Nick's existence was at stake.

"Move one more inch and your ass is mine. Try me. I've got nothing to lose," a fierce masculine voice warned.

In an instant the tone registered.

"Nick?" I whispered.

Nothing. Silence.

"Nick. Nicholas Winters," I said again, but a lot firmer and louder this time.

"Jill?" the voice questioned.

Moving in front of Liam, a calculated risk was made. Boldly marching into the kitchen, my concern over potentially being shot, stabbed, or knocked out vanished. It was a chance I had to take. Too much time had passed since Nick disappeared. If he was on the other side of the wall another second wouldn't be spared.

A shocked gasp escaped my lungs the moment the space came into clear focus. It was Nick, alive and well, dressed in all white, clean shaven, practically bald, and holding one hell of a huge knife. Dropping the weapon upon realizing the situation was safe, he took hold of my body, clinging to it tightly. Relief like I never experienced before caused my frame to buckle at the knees. The nightmare was finally over.

Chapter 16

Nick

The second I heard Jillian's voice I truly thought my mind was playing tricks on me. It wasn't until she made her way into the kitchen with her hands up at her sides that my brain believed this was for real. Grabbing her, I gripped her slender figure, holding it close. The emotion was indescribable. However, as quickly as happiness entered my once lifeless core, it vanished twice as fast.

"You've got to get the hell out of here, immediately, Jill," I urged.

"Not without you," she demanded. "Let's go. Lessor is in town at a hardware store with his cousin. We have time, but not a lot."

"Move your asses. We can sort through all of the details later," Liam said, coming into view from where Jillian had initially hid.

"Besides you two, who else is here?" I asked, concerned over how many others might be in the direct line of fire.

"Just us," Jillian answered, tugging on my left arm, and pulling me to the back door.

"There are others being held here – taken, like me. We have to get them out too, Jill. They're sick and need help."

"How many and what type of *sick* are we talking

about? Can they move on their own?" Liam questioned.

"Aside from me, seventeen others, both male and female, varying in age. Physically they're healthy, mentally they're suffering from Stockholm Syndrome, as well as a host of other issues. They trust me. I've been helping them, holding sessions, but they won't go willingly."

"Where are they now?" Liam inquired.

"All over the house – first floor and basement. Only one is on the second level."

"Round them up," Liam instructed.

Leaving Jillian and Liam in the kitchen, I sprinted to the staircase, the most central point of the house. "I need everyone in the kitchen straightaway. This is an emergency," I shouted at the top of my lungs. Within seconds the entire "flock" rushed to where I stood.

"Is this a new Brother and Sister?" Ruth queried.

"Yes. This is Brother Liam and Sister Jill. They only arrived a few moments ago, but they came with an important, dire message. We need to get out of this house as fast as possible. We're in danger. I trust them. You should too," I said.

Sarah approached from the right, clinging to my side. Her suspicious brown eyes sized my wife up. "No," she replied calmly. "I'm not going anywhere and neither can you. You're my special partner and you will be punished by God if you abandon me."

"Sarah, I need you to listen carefully. Now is not the time for this. You must have faith in me when I tell you, and all of our family, we must go," I explained.

Confusion spread amongst the "flock." None of them were sure of what to do or whom to listen to. Most began experiencing panic attacks while the others stood frozen in a state of shock. There was no way I'd be able to convince them to leave freely.

"Jill, phone," I barked, waving my hand at her. Taking her device, I dialed nine-one-one.

"Nine-one-one. What's your emergency?" a female operator asked.

"My name is Nicholas Winters. I was abducted. There are seventeen others who were as well. Our captor is Warren Lessor. He's away from the house with his cousin, Noah Lessor. I don't know when they'll return, but they will in the near future. We're in danger. Please send help."

"Do you have an address, sir?" the operator inquired.

"I'm unsure of what it is, but," I started to say before Sarah pounced, knocking the phone out of my hand.

"No," she shrieked, tackling me to the floor.

"Sarah, stop," I shouted, attempting to subdue her without causing her bodily harm.

"You're mine. If we leave, you won't be. They'll rip us apart and I won't let that happen," Sarah screamed. The chef's knife I'd dropped earlier was currently being wielded in my face.

"Think about what you're doing. What you're saying, Sarah," I said, lowering my tone, finally able to take hold of her wrists, and pushing them with all my might against the tile floor. The weapon rested beside her head.

"I am. If we die together, we'll always be together."

From where I was on the floor my view was obscured by Sarah's frame. I didn't see Jillian approaching from the side. What I did observe was Sarah's body ripped out from under mine. The force was so strong my grip instantly released. By the time I could get on my feet, Jillian had her slammed against the wall.

"I don't know what the hell is going on here, but what I can tell you is Nick Winters is *my* husband and he's leaving right now. I'll be damned if he's not getting out of this freak show, house of horrors with me today. You can stay if you'd like, but if you ever try to hurt him again, I will end you. Am I making myself clear, you fucking psychotic freak?" she threatened. Jill's eyes were wide and white as her hands shook from the force used to keep Sarah in place.

The "flock" simply stood, staring, unsure of how to develop the morning's events. After a pregnant pause, six made a break out of the front door. Liam chased after them. Releasing her hold on Sarah, Jillian approached the others.

"I'm sorry if I scared you, but what Sarah just did wasn't all right. I'm going to level with you. I'm Nick's wife. His *real* wife. The man who brought you all here, Warren Lessor, abducted you, which is illegal. You may like living in this house with him and all your friends, but this isn't a healthy or safe environment. I promise, there's no need to worry or stress out. I won't allow anything bad to happen to any of you. This is a scary situation, I understand that, but the same way Nick wants to help you is the same way I do too. I'm asking a lot, I know, but please, trust me," Jillian spoke kindly.

"Jill is a safe person," I assured. "She's your friend. She won't harm you."

The terrified, beyond frightened expressions staring back at Jill and I spoke volumes. Some latched onto others while the rest simply remained frozen in place.

"There's no protection out there from the sinners,

Brother Nicholas," Sean, a middle-aged man, rationalized. His voice trembled. His limbs shook. How he remained in the upright position would always be an unsolved mystery.

"You have me, Brother Sean. You will always have me," I comforted.

"What will happen to us? What will happen to Brothers Warren and Noah?" Sean inquired. The wheels were turning inside of his head. Answering his questions with kid gloves was key or else he'd remain in place. "You'll be free from Brother Warren's hold. You'll be able to experience life in a healthier, happier way. I realize your pasts were traumatic, abusive, and filled with negative hardships, but I will personally make sure you receive the help and assistance required to get better, stronger, and empowered so you can move on and find true, pure happiness and fulfillment. As for Warren and Noah, they'll be given the same opportunities as all of you. Don't worry about them. Focus on yourselves and your own needs. It's okay to do that. Self-care and self-love are not selfish acts." The "flock" split fifty/fifty. Half refused to listen. The rest were onboard.

"Let's take this slow, as a group. We'll all walk out of the front door, together, and see how we feel," I suggested.

One by one they lined up, including the ones who resisted the change, even Sarah. Guiding them from the kitchen to the front porch felt like a million-mile journey. It appeared Liam had wrangled the runners and had them sitting on the ground, leaning against his car. He spoke with them, but exactly what he said, I couldn't hear. They were six less to worry about.

Chapter 17

Liam

Up until Nick all but demanded we help the other abductees inside of the house, things appeared to be going smoothly. Stupidly, I believed the stroke of luck – finding Nick alive and well had all the makings of a happily-ever-after fairytale. To be honest, and please forgive me if I come across as an uncaring dick, between the nine-one-one call Nick placed before his psycho cult life partner tackled him *and* with Jillian's spy pin broadcasting all over social media sites, if we left the others behind they would've eventually been rescued. The whole point of this suicide mission was to save Nick, *not* liberate the world. But, never-the-less, here we were. An overweight, out of shape, smoker chasing six lunatics dressed in white down a rural country road in the freezing cold. If anyone were viewing this as an outsider with no prior knowledge of the current setup, it would've resembled a mental institution breakout. All that was missing was me wielding a butterfly net. Panting, knees on fire, I kept booking it, screaming for them to stop – which, spoiler alert, they did not. Finally, I was able to catch up to one of the slower ones, wrestling his chubby body to the ground. Once this happened, the others stopped. They turned, then approached me in a circular, confrontational fashion.

"Look, I'm not trying to hurt any of you. In fact, it's the exact opposite. Just hear me out," I explained, helping the man to his feet while clutching the stitch in my side. The words were met with confused stares.

"I have no idea what happened before and after Lessor abducted you people, but I'm going to take a wild guess and say that it was pretty severe and mentally damaging. You're scared, hurt, disoriented – I get it. There's a choice to be made, though. Right here. Right now. You can keep running or we can take a nice calm walk back to the house and share a pleasant chat. Either way, the police will find you. I can't stress enough – no one is in trouble. Nobody is going to jail. Nothing bad is going to happen. You're safe. I promise. I wouldn't lie," I said, finally being able to breathe normally again.

The six formed a huddle. Hushed whispers filled their private space. Not being able to hear what was being said irritated me, but quite frankly, if they decided to make another run for it, I had zero intentions of going after them. I'd call Jamison and have him keep a lookout – they wouldn't be too hard to spot, and inform the cops whenever they decided to show up. It wasn't as if they had many options. The road extended for miles, void of heavily trafficked areas. The authorities would be able to locate them with ease. After a few moments, I spoke again.

"Guys, it's the easy way or the dirt road."

"Will you protect us if Brother Warren finds us or sees us walking back to the house? He will be mad. We're not supposed to leave the property," a somewhat young Asian woman asked.

"Of course," I assured.

"What happens when the police arrive?" she

pressed. Apparently, she was the spokesperson for the group.

"They'll want to speak with each of you to find out what happened. Again, nobody is in trouble. The cops will not be arresting anyone. They have absolutely no reason to."

"Where will they take us? Back to our old homes?" Her voice trembled when suggesting she, or any of them, might have to return to their old lives.

"Probably to the hospital for a checkup to make sure you're all okay and healthy. From there, I don't know. What I can offer is if your home lives were abusive or bad in any way, tell the police and the hospital staff. They won't make you return to a harmful situation. There are places all over the state to assist people enduring circumstances such as yourselves." I paused. "Listen, it's freezing cold out here. None of you have coats on. I don't know when Lessor and his cousin will come driving down that road or when the cops will get here for that matter. Let's start walking back to the house. We can sort everything out there. Sound like a plan?"

The group shot glances back and forth before nodding.

"Okay," the Asian woman replied, drawing closer to my side.

With that, we began the journey back. In an attempt to keep moral up and to avoid a sudden change of heart moment where they might take off like a bat out of Hell again, I began talking about myself. I told them about my career, family, hobbies, and things of the sort. Four of the six engaged, the other two kept silent. As long as they stayed with the pack, I could've cared less. On the surface they came across as simple, kind individuals.

Hopefully, once this was over, they'd receive the necessary treatment to deprogram and heal so they could go on to live happy, fulfilling existences. Upon reaching the apron of the driveway, I didn't see Nick or Jillian outside.

Damn it!

Not wanting to leave the six defectors alone and having no desire to re-enter the house, I lined them up against my car where an easy eye could be kept on them. My gut instinct suggested all of them would adhere to the directive to not move, but who the hell really knew? Eventually Nick and Jillian would have to exit the home, but if they didn't, the cops could go in and deal with it. Don't get me wrong, I felt deeply for each and every single person who'd been abducted, but a scenario like this was out of my scope of knowledge. All I could do was pray the police would show up before Lessor, and we'd be long gone before the shit hit the fan. Out of the corner of my eye, I spotted Nick, Jillian, and the others all in a line, and heading in my direction.

"See? There's Nick. He'll be able to answer any questions you may have better than I can," I said, thanking God the two finally moved their asses, were safe, and close by.

Dear Lord, please get me the hell out of here as fast and safely as you can.

"What's the plan, Jill?" I heard Nick whisper.

"Between your nine-one-one call and the live feed I'm streaming, it shouldn't be too long before help arrives," she answered.

"What if Warren comes back before then?" I spoke up.

"We deal with it. We'll have to buy time," Jillian

replied.

"My ass, Jill. We're playing with fire. If that nut cake returns and we're all standing around blowing up his spot he's going to flip out. There's no way I'm sticking around to find out what happens next, and neither should you. Don't you realize how dangerous this is? This isn't a movie. It's real life," I rationalized, attempting to remain calm, but failing miserably. The position we were in was no joking matter. Too many lives were at stake due to too many unknown variables.

"Then what do you suggest we do?" she countered.

"We get the hell out of here as rapidly as possible. We can call the authorities once we're back on the main road. If anyone requires immediate medical attention, we'll take them with us, but I can't squeeze everyone inside of my car." My God, why was this turning into a debate? Why was I the only one who had any common sense, any healthy logic of fear?

Before Nick or Jillian had a chance to respond, the sound of gravel crunching under heavy tires sliced through the thin, frosty air. Glancing to the left, a tan van slowly rolled up the driveway. An older gentleman drove, while a younger one sat in the passenger seat. It had to be Lessor and his cousin.

"Oh, you've got to be kidding me," I hissed under my breath.

Sorry. You lose, Liam. Better luck next time ... if there even will be a next time. Get down, stay low, and pray like you've never prayed before. Shit is about to get real – fast.

Chapter 18

Nick

"Crap," I hissed.

"Brother Warren! Brother Warren!" Sarah called. Her hands waved wildly above her head as she ran into his arms. "Brother Nicholas and these two sinners are *forcing* us to leave. The girl says she's his *wife*, but she's *not* because *I* am. He called the police and she assaulted me. They say you're evil and we need to run far away from you and Noah."

"What?" Warren shouted, taking her by the shoulders and giving her a good, solid shake. His body language reflected true, raw alarm; panic in its purest form. "Did you do this? Did you invite these outsiders, these sinners, into my home?"

"I did. You're sick, Warren. You need help," I said, approaching him cautiously.

"What have you done?" he gasped.

"It's over. The police are on their way. If you let these people go, individuals you had no right to take in the first place, the authorities will go easier on you. I'll make sure you're placed in a facility where you can get better, and I'll do everything in my power to ensure that your punishment isn't as severe as it technically speaking should be." Remaining calm proved simpler than I had expected.

"You betrayed me. After all I've done for you," he raged. Opening the passenger side door of the van, he yanked Noah out by his right shoulder, shoving him to the ground. From my vantage point all I could make out was him digging around inside of the vehicle for something. Seconds later he stood before me, aiming a gun at my chest.

"It doesn't have to be like this. Do you really think this is what God wants you to do? Murder another human being? Who'd be the sinner then?" Inhaling deeply, I knew, in this moment, fear could not be a factor. Warren encompassed the ability to kill another without guilt, but if I kept him talking for a few more minutes, by then the police should be here and would defuse the situation using force I wasn't privy to.

"I'm God, you idiot. What I say goes. My will. My desires. Not yours. Not theirs." His eyes went wild as his frame tightened. An eerie smirk spread across his thin lips. His head curtly jerked from side to side. He'd lost it. Anything occurring after this point would be a true, honest act of insanity.

"All right, God. Tell me, why have you done this? Why haven't you used your almighty power to assist others on a broader level?"

Keep him talking. Make him think. The moment he stops you're screwed and dead. Jillian, Liam, and everyone else, too.

"I thought you were smarter. Obviously, I stand corrected," he balked. "Never once did I lay a finger on anybody living in this house. No harm ever came to them. I protected, loved, and guided them. I showed them mercy and the way to salvation. I did the same for you. With time, our community grew, and would've

168

continued to if not for you, but all hope isn't lost. You see, I anticipated something like this happening. One day I knew a wolf in sheep's clothing would do this to me, to us. This gun has eight bullets, and there's only three of you. Even if I miss, I'll still have extras to spare. Once you're out of the equation, my family will keep going. Only a true moron wouldn't have a contingency plan. What's the strategy, you ask? That's my business. The best part? You'll never find out because you'll be dead, and no one will ever find your bodies. Eventually, society will erase you from their memories. The world will be free of three more ingrates, and I will be hailed a king among men."

Inching closer, the cold steal of the handgun pressed against my neck. It's funny how you never feel as alive as you do when you're moments away from death. Locking eyes with Warren, I took a breath. One false move and his finger could slip, ending me.

"You're a freaking deranged psycho," Jillian said. Absolute disgust dripped off each accusatory word.

"And you're a nasty, dirty whore," he sneered.

The second his focus shifted away from me and onto Jillian, I shoved him to the ground.

BANG!

Liam fell. His body slid down the side of his Subaru.

BANG!

A forceful pressure slammed into my left arm. The impact birthed a pain so unreal, my consciousness faded in and out within seconds of the impact.

BANG!

BANG!

My brain desperately wanted to make sure Jillian was okay, but couldn't focus long enough on anything.

Before a blanket of darkness covered my soul, controlling my thoughts and movements, or rather lack thereof, the blaring sound of sirens sliced through the air. My extremities iced over. A hazy cloud of blurriness stung my eyes. Then, nothing.

Chapter 19

Jillian

Growing up with a gun enthusiast father, I'd held all different types of weapons, but had never fired one at anything other than a stationary, non-living or breathing object. Today, I did – twice, and without a second thought. However, the people watching my live stream witnessed it too, but I had no other choice. Nick shoved Lessor. His weapon went off accidently nailing Liam in the right leg. With a wail of anguish, Liam dropped like a ton of bricks. The gun fell. Sarah picked it up, firing a round at Nick, making contact with his left shoulder. To describe what transpired inside of my core at that very moment would be like trying to catch smoke with your bare hands – impossible. There were too many thoughts to process at once. Too many choices to make in an instant. A ruthless darkness arose within my soul. The Devil within me came out. Charging Sarah without fear of being shot, I punched her in the jaw with the strength of one hundred men. She let go of the weapon while crashing into the hard gravel driveway. I grabbed the gun and turned to find Lessor getting to his feet. Lumbering in my direction, he spewed a string of obscenity laced threats. He kept coming at me. You'd think I'd freeze up, crap, I thought I would as well, but I didn't.

"I'm going to make you regret you were ever born,

you disgusting whore. Roast in hell, sinner bitch," he screamed while attempting to remove the gun from my hand.

A brief struggle ensued, but one swift knee to the groin and he backed way the hell up, doubling over. Still in possession of the weapon, my fingers wrapped around the trigger, firing blindly. His pupils widened. His body stammered backwards while his hands clutched his chest. Blood dripped from his mouth before he fell.

"No!" Sarah shrieked. Scrambling to her feet she ran at me.

Without prompting, my arms rose, and my fingers pulled the trigger again. The impact occurred on her right foot. She dropped beside Lessor's stiff, motionless body. His mouth was agape and his eyes were wide open. He was dead. There was no doubt about it.

Seconds later, the authorities arrived. Dozens of emergency medical vehicles flooded the property. Everything from that point on until later that night was a haze. All I can clearly recall was being told to drop the weapon and to put my hands up – to which I complied. I wasn't allowed to ride with Nick in the ambulance – a paramedic forced me into my own. Once at the hospital, I was wheeled on a gurney from one room to another, never seeing or speaking with the same doctor or nurse twice. I kept asking about Nick, but was either ignored or told he was okay, which I didn't believe because no one would let me see him to confirm this. Finally, after being diagnosed with shock and a broken left hand, I was told I was being discharged. Exiting the exam room, my hand now casted, I saw Kendra sitting on a bench, alone. Her expression was a mix of rage, anxiety, and worry.

"Jill," she exclaimed, instantly rising, and

embracing me tightly.

"I'm so sorry, Kendra," I cried. Blocked emotions broke free. Tears flowed as my body shook. Fear of the unknown rose to the surface.

"Liam is going to be fine. The bullet grazed his thigh. It's only a flesh wound that will require a few stitches. The nurse said it looks worse than it really is. He will be out shortly. Nick has been in surgery for the past three hours. He lost a lot of blood, but last I heard the doctors were able to remove the entire bullet and are now working to fix the mess of bones, muscles, and tendons in his shoulder. How are you? Are you okay?" She forced my body to sit beside hers.

"I don't know," I replied, because the truth was, I didn't. Kendra's words made sense and were positive, but until I saw him face to face, got to speak with him, I wouldn't believe anything I was told.

"I saw what happened, Jill. You weren't wrong for shooting those two lunatics."

Her kindness meant the world to me, but I wasn't in the headspace to receive it. Instead, I hugged her, whispering another apology. "I'm so sorry for dragging you and Liam into this," I wept.

"It's all right, Jill. Everyone is going to be just fine."

"Mrs. Winters?" a man's voice inquired.

"Yes," I replied, pulling away from Kendra. Agent Wilder came into view.

"I need to speak with you to get your statement."

"Go. I'll wait here. If I hear anything at all, I'll come get you," Kendra replied, squeezing my good hand tightly.

Nodding, I got up and trailed Wilder down a hallway and into an empty exam room.

"I just spoke with Doctor Harrison. He said Doctor Winters should be in the recovery room shortly, and the surgery went better than expected." Wilder took a seat on the bed. He reached for the rolling tray table and pulled it closer to where he sat. A beat-up notebook slammed against the plastic surface. Licking his right thumb and index fingers, he flipped through the pages until a blank one presented.

"I think all doctors say that. Makes them appear to be heroes to the worried families in the waiting room," I said, standing in the farthest corner I could located that was away from him. A rather large part of me felt that in a few minutes he'd been slapping silver bracelets on my wrists for committing murder, twice.

"You know? I think you're right. Anyway, if you're feeling up to it, could you walk me through what happened? I saw the live feed, but I need your personal, eyewitness statement."

"I'm not saying a word without my lawyer present, nor will I give any sort of recollection of events until I see my husband."

"Charles Downey?"

"Yes."

"I'll give him a call right away, but you cannot leave this hospital until we speak. Are we clear?"

"Crystal," I answered, exiting the room, and heading back to Kendra, who was speaking with a man in scrubs. Liam was beside her, propped up on crutches.

"This is Nick's wife, Jillian Winters," Kendra informed.

"Mrs. Winters, I'm Doctor Harrison. I performed your husband's surgery. He's doing well and is currently in a step-down unit. Nick sustained a gunshot wound to the left shoulder. I was able to remove the entire bullet and the damage caused was repairable. Nothing major was touched. There was substantial blood loss, but two transfusions were administered. He'll be here for a few days, but I expect a full recovery. Physical therapy will be key in the healing process, however we'll discuss follow-up care later. He's been asking for you. If you'd like, I can take you back to see him, but only for a few minutes. Nick needs to rest. However, I must warn you. He's on a lot of pain medication and is coming down from the anesthesia, so he's in and out of it quite a bit."

"Thank you. I'd like to see him, please."

"Of course. If you'll follow me."

Hot on his heals, I kept up with his rapid pace, walking through a series of several doors before seeing Nick lying on a bed. Rushing to his side, I inspected him not only visually, but with my hands as well. His shoulder had been wrapped and placed in a sling. In all our years together I'd never seen him appear as weak or small. His skin tone was ashy. His eyelids were slick and slightly swollen.

"Babe?" he whispered weakly.

"I'm right here, Nick. How do you feel?" I asked, lacing his fingers with mine.

"Fine. Ask me when the pain killers wear off." He chuckled. "What happened to your hand? Are you all right?"

"I'm good. Don't worry about me."

"You saved my life, Jill."

"Shhh. Get some sleep. I'll sit here with you until they kick me out. When you get into a room, I'll be there. I'll call Lyla and have her bring up some things from the house. If there's something you'd like, let me know. The doctor says you'll be here for a few days." Focusing on anything other than celebrating Nick being okay wasn't comprehendible. My emotions would have to wait until later. Right now, Nick needed me to be the rock, his rock, the same way he'd been mine since day one.

"I love you, babe," he sighed before his eyes shut.

"I love you more."

Chapter 20

Nick

My hospital stay was one giant blur. Most of it was spent high as a kite on pain meds, which I was beyond grateful for. When the weaning process started, discomfort kicked up in full force. Jillian remained by my side, tending to my every need, want, or desire. What she'd done for me...the image caused a giant lump to form in my throat every time it popped into my brain. Not wanting to discuss what happened while abducted, I denied psychological treatment, suggesting I'd seek counseling privately upon discharge. However, curiosity pertaining to what happened to Warren, Noah, and the "flock" consumed my thoughts. One afternoon, when Jillian went down to the cafeteria to grab lunch, I asked one of the nurses. Though she shouldn't have shared the information, my charm persuaded her otherwise strong ethical judgement.

They'd been spread out among several psychiatric hospitals on Long Island and in Queens where they'd remain in inpatient programs, Noah included. The treating physicians here felt separating them would be the best course of action. I humbly disagreed with the approach, but it wasn't my call to make. Sarah had been shot by Jillian in the foot, and was shipped off to a rehab center in Brooklyn where she'd be able to heal physically and mentally in a state-of-the-art facility. There was a chance she'd never be able to use the limb again. The bullet shattered all the bones, but her doctor was hopeful. As for Warren, Jillian killed him. He bled out in the driveway of his compound. A clean shot to the stomach. By the time he arrived at the hospital, he'd already passed.

"Ready to go home?" Jillian asked brightly about a week after the incident.

"Yes. Please. Get me out of here," I replied, thrilled to be sprung from this joint. I hadn't seen the inside of my house in months and couldn't wait to kick back and relax in my own bed after taking a nice, long, hot shower. "Hey, Jill."

"Yeah?" she answered distracted. Her eyes were scanning the room to make sure she'd packed everything.

Approaching her from the side, my good arm reached for her shoulder. "When we're back home and settled in, we need to talk. Let's do this right this time. Okay?"

"We don't have to, Nick. Yes, I have questions, but after what you've gone through if you don't want to discuss it, we can let it go. I get it. To be honest, you should probably speak to someone about this. Someone who can help you navigate the aftermath better than I'm equipped to. I'm here for you. I love you. We're good. What happened, what you had to say or do in order to survive..." her voice trailed. To keep up the appearance she was okay and strong for not only her, but for me as well, she fought like hell to keep her tears from flowing. Shaking her head, she shoved the rise of emotions far away. "We've got this, Nick." Moist, sapphire eyes locked with mine. I couldn't have loved her more than I did in that moment.

"Come here, babe," I said, holding my one good arm out against her waist.

Accepting the gesture, she inhaled deeply, burying her head in my neck. "Though I know you're tremendously saddened I won't be driving," she started, holding up her casted hand, "a car should be here by now. There will be a crap ton of press outside waiting for us to leave, so Charles is meeting us in the lobby. He arraigned for security to get us the hell out of here without a huge shit show scene."

Since the escape, the media went wild. Not feeling up to listening to all of the reports, Jillian and I chose to ignore the stories. The comically wild ones that Liam had forwarded us allowed us to share a good laugh, but the rest, neither of us had a need for. The police and FBI came in and out of my room at all times of the day and night asking the same questions over and over again. My major concern was for Jillian. She'd shot and killed Warren and had caused potentially permanent damage to Sarah. Though Jillian said she wasn't worried, she was. Her lawyer spent quite a bit of time up here as well. When all was said and done, no charges were brought against her. Warren's death and Sarah's injuries were considered acts of self-defense.

Visitors were limited to a select few to avoid turning the hospital into a three-ring circus. Not so shocking, my parents and siblings came by armed with a full camera crew, which to their dismay wasn't allowed inside. They stayed for a short while – maybe twenty minutes at the longest. I kept the conversation light, not saying much. Jillian disappeared when they showed up, but I couldn't blame her. Apparently, my abduction had made great news for the Winters Family, putting their name back into the headlines.

"My attorneys will schedule a press conference for the morning you're released," my father said, patting my injured shoulder, then actively ignoring the wince of pain he'd inflicted on me. "We'll film it downstairs in the main entrance lobby. When it's over, we'll get into the limo as a family. The press will go wild over it."

"That won't be necessary. I'm fine, don't need the attention, and want to put this behind me and Jill."

"Don't be stupid, son. This is just what Jackson needs to boost his numbers in the polls. A good, strong showing of household solidarity. We'll all be there, but it's best to leave your wife out of this. After all, she shot that woman and killed that man. That's not the image we want to put out there."

"Absolutely not. My wife put her ass on the line to get me back. What she had to do, what she went through far surpasses anything any one of you have ever done for me. Jill committed murder, something which will haunt her every waking dream for all eternity, to bring me home. Would any of you ever even considered doing something like that for someone you love? No, no you wouldn't. Not everything is about ratings, good stories, and free publicity. This is my personal business we're talking about. I just experienced the most horrific event of my entire life, and all you're concerned with is Jackson, who's standing in the corner, barely making eye contact with or speaking to me other than saying, 'Hey,' when he walked in, but who's totally fine. I was shot – with a frigging bullet, for Christ's sake. Before that, I was abducted. Kept locked away in a freaking house of horrors. The things Jill and I had to do to escape that, you'd have never." I paused, taking a deep breath. "Thank you for coming by. I appreciate the time. I'll reach out when I get home and am feeling better."

"Not everything is about you and that wife of yours, Nicholas," my mother said very matter-of-factly.

"This time it was, Mom, but in your eyes it never is."

They lingered for a few short moments before making an excuse – something about having to check in on my grandfather who'd fallen under the weather a few weeks ago, and left.

Good Riddance.

What would happen next? Who knew. Recent events had caused an overflow of doubt and queries within me. I felt I failed Warren's "flock." I should've been able to help them, heal them, but I hadn't. Decades of learning and acquired knowledge were called into question. How could I keep writing books, giving lectures, hosting a Podcast dispensing useless, if not dangerous advice? I truly believed myself to be a fraud. An empty, hopelessness settled inside of my gut.

"Everything heals, Nick. Body, mind, and soul – it all gets better, happier, stronger, it just takes time," Jillian urged, and she was right.

"My mind's all over the place, Jill," I admitted. It had been some time since I opened up to her about my personal internal struggles. Usually I played the role of the rock. The reversal felt weird, causing me to feel weak and helpless.

"It has every reason to be, but instead of going back to what we've always done, why not start over? New house. New careers. New perspective on life. New everything, Nick. I'm not saying we run away from the past. I'm saying we run in another direction. Seasons change four times a year and no one says a damn thing. Why can't we make one bold transformation together?" She shrugged.

"I don't know, Jill."

"Well, you're in luck because I do," she replied, reaching for my hand and walking us out of the room, thus ending not only a chapter of our lives, but completing the entire book.

Chapter 21

Jillian

One Year Later...

"Tonight's "End Game" segment is going to be a little different and emotional for me. As many of you already know, this will be my final *The Bottom Line* broadcast. It's no secret my husband, Nick, and I are expecting our first child in three months, but what we haven't announced yet, what I'm beyond thrilled to share is starting in the coming weeks on this network, Nick and I will be cohosting our own live morning talk show called, *This Just In.* I wanted to take this time to thank my viewing audience for welcoming me into their homes every night, for placing unwavering trust in my ability to provide accurate, unbiased news, and for weathering all of the storms experienced here without judgement, but rather with constant support. I am sad to leave, but excited to start this new chapter. I'd also like to thank the entire crew who've gone above and beyond each and every single day to make sure they deliver the best show to you. My producer, Liam Steven, will be joining Nick and me on the new set, as well as my personal assistant, Lyla Marx. Topher Robbins, our station owner, has something special up his sleeve for this time slot beginning tomorrow. After the show closes tonight, a trailer for *This Just In* will introduce you to our new morning format, as well as allow Mr. Robbins an opportunity to fill you in on everything in between. Nick, Liam, Lyla, Mr. Robbins, our crew, myself, and baby girl Winters all hope you'll make us part of your morning wakeup routine. As for now, for the last time, I'm Jillian Winters, and that's the bottom line. Goodnight."

"Cut, and we're out," Liam shouted, removing his headset. "Great show everyone. Thank you."

Usually I'd jump out of my chair to stretch, but tonight I sat motionless as tears fell freely from my eyes. It was the end of a career-making era. That moment between old and new, comfortable and uncertainty.

"Hey. You okay, Jill?" Liam asked, leaning against the anchor desk.

"Stupid pregnancy hormones," I lied, wiping the moisture away with the tips of my fingers.

"It's almost over. Then you're in for a totally new adventure." He laughed. "The crew got a goodbye cake for you. It's your favorite – chocolate mousse. Come on, no more tears." Pulling me up and into a warm embrace, he softly patted my back.

"One last thing," I said, taking my cell phone off of the tabletop. Clicking open the picture app, I snapped a quick selfie of us before vacating my old set.

A lot had changed in the short year following Nick's abduction. At first, it was a rough ride. Nick suffered extreme highs and lows, until one day he seemed to level off. That was the day I told him we were pregnant. Everything inside of him did a one-hundred-eighty degree turn. Life had returned to his core. Aspects from attitude to appearance transformed in an instant back to his old self. He'd been seeing a therapist to work through the PTSD and severity of what happened. Truthfully? I'd been seeing one too. On the outside it came across as we were both finally moving forward from the past – which we were, but we both had a keen awareness more needed to change before we could shed all of the previous year's hauntings.

The idea for the morning show was pitched by Liam, which came at precisely the right time. Nick had made a decision to take a step back from all things psychology, giving up his book deal and Podcast, and was searching for something else to fill his days with. The beginning of my pregnancy was filled with terrible morning, noon, and night sickness causing me to be too ill to tape a live show some nights. Liam suggested Nick fill in. Since the idea came from him, Topher quickly agreed to it. The seamless transition between Nick's time and mine grew popular among viewers, practically doubling the station's nightly rankings. Added bonus, Nick loved anchoring. Though his approach differed from mine, he maintained the heart and soul of the program in my absence. To test his hypothesis if Nick and I should do a show together, every Friday we'd co-host *The Bottom Line*. Ratings went through the roof. Halfway through Liam's morning talk show pitch, Topher signed on the dotted line. In one month we'd be embarking upon a new journey, together. It also didn't hurt that after the abduction, and after millions of people had watched the Warren Lessor takedown live feed, Nick and I quickly became America's favorite couple. Any negative press we had received in the past was erased, totally forgotten from the court of public opinion's memories. The moment news of my pregnancy hit the press we became untouchable. Golden.

We did end up moving to another gated community on Long Island. A house we paid for, not a gift from his family. Once the old property sold, Nick wrote a check to his parents, thus severing ties with them. No longer feeling indebted to his family, a weight lifted off of his shoulders. He did, however, keep in contact with Beau. During quiet hours in the dead of night when I couldn't sleep, my mind often wondered exactly what role the Winters played in his abduction. My gut suggested Beau had something to do with it, but I couldn't figure out exactly what. Eventually I let it go because they no longer mattered, but the musing remained dormant. It probably always would.

Our new home and joint career path were the perfect start in regaining the lost balance between us, and to be honest, life was good. Neither of us had any complaints. Finally done with the unpacking and nursery setup, we crashed on the couch together, exhausted, one Saturday afternoon.

"Would you totally hate me if I asked you to get me a chocolate raspberry shake from that ice cream place down the street?" I asked. Pregnancy cravings were consuming most days.

"Are you going to want it this time when I get back? Yesterday you had me running all over the world for things and when I got home you wanted none of it, then got mad at me when I ate it." Nick laughed.

"I think the words you're looking for are, 'Thank you *so* much, Jill, for carrying my baby, and for doing all of the heavy lifting while I sit around waiting to drive you to the hospital.'" I smirked.

"Is there anything else you'd like?" Nick smiled, leaning over, and kissing my lips.

Before I could answer, the doorbell chimed.

"Are you expecting anyone?" I asked, sitting straighter.

"No," he replied, getting up and going to the front door. Joining him, I peered out of the side window. A young man dressed in a dark brown delivery uniform stood, glancing at his watch. Turning the brass doorknob, Nick greeted the courier.

"Are you Doctor Nicholas Winters?" The man inquired.

"Yes," Nick replied. "How can I help you?"

"This is for you. If I could please get your signature here, I'd greatly appreciate it."

"May I ask whom this is from?"

"I'm not sure, sir. I work for Line Runners Logistics. They give me a truck and a route every morning. I just deliver the items to whomever they're addressed to."

"Of course," Nick said, taking the stylus and quickly scribbling his initials on the courier's tablet.

After signing, the courier handed over a large, manila envelope. Thanking the man and closing the door, he examined the enclosure. Aside from Nick's full name written in perfect cursive with a thick, black permanent marker, nothing else was on it. No return address. Nothing. He slid his index finger under the sealed flap. A single thick slice of pure white paper fell out into his hand.

An ominous, dark sensation slowly crept up my spine and back down to my gut, sitting like a lead weight. Call it intuition, instinct – whatever you want, but the letter radiated pure evil.

"What does it say? Who is it from?" I questioned as I bit down hard on my left thumb nail.

Clearing his throat, Nick read, " 'This they said, tempting him that they might have to accuse him. But Jesus stooped down, and with his finger wrote on the ground, as though he heard them not. So, when they continued asking him, he lifted up himself, and said unto them, He that is without sin among you, let him first cast a stone at her.' – John 8: 6–7. We're not done, Brother Nicholas. Far from it."

A word about the author...

A lifelong storyteller, JP Barry specializes in crafting heart stopping, compelling, unique, emotional page turners for a variety of genres. A New York native, Barry is always on the hunt for ideas for her next novel. When not writing, Barry enjoys spending time with her family.